Positive Impacts is very understandable and applicable to nearly anyone in the modern workplace. Dr. Hissong has placed a great emphasis on real world examples that guide the reader through the considerable range of concepts addressed in the book.

Conceptually, I found *Positive Impacts* to have the range of coverage as many other popular books in the field, but the readability and "lagniappe" make this book a super choice for anyone needing fast directions in the changing world of workplace relationships.

C. B. Crawford, Ph.D.
Center for Interdisciplinary Studies
Fort Hays State University

Finally comes a book that demystifies the dynamics of interpersonal communication! *Positive Impacts* is filled with familiar situations, stories, and anecdotes to explain how to improve communication skills.

The book covers a wide range of valuable topics, such as creating motivation, listening, and effective management styles. The author also gives pointers for effective written, telephone, and e-mail communication.

Positive Impacts is not a business manual, but a primer of basic rules for interpersonal communication that were part of the unwritten curriculum of childhood playtime. Sadly, many of us didn't learn these guidelines during our hours in the sandbox, but there is still time!

This book should be required reading for students and professionals of all disciplines, as well as anyone who wants to be more effective in day-to-day interpersonal communications.

Tara L. Kuther, Ph.D.
Assistant Professor of Psychology
Western Connecticut State University

Positive Impacts

Discovering the Keys to Better Interpersonal and Communication Skills

Positive Impacts

Discovering the Keys to Better Interpersonal and Communication Skills

by Doug Hissong

BONNEVILLE BOOKS™

Springville, Utah

ISBN: 1-55517-582-1
v.1

Published by Bonneville Books
Imprint of Cedar Fort Inc.
www.cedarfort.com

Distributed by:

Typeset by Kristin Nelson
Cover design by Adam Ford
Cover design © 2001 by Lyle Mortimer

Printed in the United States of America
10 9 8 7 6 5 4 3 2 1

Printed on acid-free paper

Library of Congress Cataloging-in-Publication Data

Hissong, Doug, 1942-
 Positive impacts : discovering the keys to better interpersonal and communication skills
/ by Doug Hissong.
    p. cm.
Includes bibliographical references.
 ISBN 1-55517-582-1 (pbk. : alk. paper)
1. Interpersonal relations. 2. Interpersonal communication. 3.
Social skills. I. Title.
HM1106 .H57 2002
302--dc21

                    2001006242

CONTENTS

Part 2 - Communication Skills

Part 3 - Lagniappe

Introduction

What is the most crucial factor determining your success in both your professional and personal life? While you're thinking about that, let me clarify some definitions. By "success" I mean your overall feeling that you're accomplishing what you'd like to and making important contributions. By "professional" I mean the work you do to support yourself, no matter what its nature. And, of course, "personal" refers to yourself and your relationships with those closest to you. Your professional life and your personal life do seem like two quite different entities, right? Would you think that the same factor could be crucial to success in both?

What have you come up with?

Well, I'm convinced that the most crucial factor determining our success in both our professional and personal lives is our **interpersonal and communication skills**. What do I base that on? On the professional side, I base it on what I've seen while working for over 30 years in American companies. On the personal side, I base it on what I've seen in living in the world for over 50 years. Let's consider three areas.

Companies

In a company of any size, your success depends on quality relationships with co-workers and internal and external customers. And you have to maintain those relationships with the same people for many years.

Time and time again I've seen people who have top-notch skills for doing what they were hired to do but who don't achieve the kind of success they should because they're lacking in interpersonal skills. This individual just doesn't interact with others as effectively as he could. He keeps too much to himself, doesn't do well on teams, or rubs people the wrong way. So he just doesn't accomplish as much as some other folks do. That loss of productivity hurts his employer, but, much more so, it restricts his career progress. His bosses may try some coaching, but then give up on him. The boss starts structuring his assignments so that less interaction with others is required, making him a "closet case". And that's a real shame because then he has less opportunity to practice, improve, and demonstrate improvement. It's a vicious circle, a downward spiral. Others, who may have less of the basic skills, do better and contribute more because they interact more effectively with co-workers and customers.

The other real shame you see in the workplace is the person who does really fine work but who just can't present that work in a good light when he writes something or gives a

The pronouns "he", "him", and "his" here refer to persons of either gender.talk. Anything he writes needs a lot of editing. When he gives a talk the audience just tolerates it and feels a bit sorry for him. His employer sends him to some writing and speaking courses, and does a little coaching, but then gives up on him. His bosses take over more and more of the writing and speaking tasks so that they're done well. Again, that provides less opportunity to improve, and another vicious circle begins. Others, who may have less of the basic skills, do better and contribute more because they're better able to show off what they've done.

Many businesses are suffering today. Competition in this global economy is tougher than ever. Companies large and small are finding it harder than ever to be successful, to make a profit. They're trying some new approaches, writing mission statements, implementing continuous improvement programs, focusing on their customers, emphasizing employee teamwork, and on and on. They're looking for an answer, basically a way to increase their productivity. In a general sense they know where the answer lies, because they know that the key to their productivity is their people, their employees. They say "our people are our most important resource", but how are they really managing that key resource? They're having trouble implementing any real changes. What can you do to actually make people more productive? What kind of environment do you try to establish? Why aren't the management initiatives providing more benefit? What's missing?

Individual Businesses

Individual businesses with just one or a few employees have increased immensely in recent years, particularly as a result of the Internet. Many are very successful, but many others go under. When you're on your own, you live or die by the relationships you develop with your customers and those you with whom you network. Potential new customers quickly form an impression of you, and that's more important than what you're selling. There are others they can do business with if you rub them the wrong way. Clear communication is crucial to success. And it's entirely up to you. Researchers have found that the most important factor to financiers of small businesses is their opinion of the champion. If they believe in the person behind the business they will fund it. And what do you think are the keys to how they view that champion?

Personal Relationships

The fact that at least one out of three marriages now ends in divorce is a very telling statistic. We get to choose the person we marry. Obviously, we strive to choose someone we'll be able to get along with. Clearly the incentives for getting along are great, since a broken marriage is a real pain. But still, more than one of three couples just can't do it. Why not? Why are there so many estranged relationships between family members? Those all-important relationships with our family and friends need regular attention if we are to have a truly rewarding and enjoyable life.

We all know that our relationships with others are important to us in both our professional lives and our personal lives. Yet somehow we continue to have difficulties in building relationships as well as we'd like, and we pay a price for that. Our quality of life suffers. Somehow we haven't thought it through enough. We're missing something.

Why do we have so much trouble relating to people, whether our kids, neighbors, friends, or whatever? Why are they so hard to understand? Why aren't they more like us?

We build our relationships with others by our interactions and communications with them, the subtle things we do and say (or don't do or say). Relationship-building skills are essential to success in all endeavors. No matter what you do, to do it well you have to be able to interact effectively and build effective relationships with others.

What is the key to having **positive impacts** on others, getting things accomplished through others? Focusing on how you interact and communicate.

This book deals with the very important human or **people-oriented** side of everything we do. The same interpersonal skills underpin our success in both our business or professional life and our personal life.

This book deals with relationships, **building relationships that work**, that is, relationships that accomplish what we want them to. We build our relationships with others by our daily interactions with them, the subtle things we do and say (or don't do or say). Relationship-building skills are essential to success in all endeavors. No matter what you do, to do it well you have to be able to interact effectively and build effective relationships with others.

Interpersonal skills are closely linked to communication skills, particularly when you're communicating one-on-one or in small groups. How effectively we interact with others depends on our ability to communicate openly and clearly with them. Communication skills diverge somewhat from the interpersonal path as you move up in scale. Large-group talks are less interpersonal than one-on-one or small group talking, but there's still the matter of rapport between a speaker and his or her audience. Informal written notes can play an important role interpersonal relationships. Longer written documents are less personal, but you can still offend people by something you write.

This book deals with **getting your message across**. The best ideas are worthless if we can't get others to understand and embrace them.

Interpersonal and communication skills are essential to success in all endeavors. No matter what you do, to do it well you have to be able to interact effectively and build effective relationships with co-workers and customers, and you have to be able to get your messages across to them effectively.

Part 1 of this book deals with the vital topic of interpersonal skills and does so in a way that I think you'll find entertaining as well as helpful. To the extent possible, I've shunned any textbook-like, scholarly, or preachy treatment in favor of anecdotes, stories, personal experiences, and analogies that illustrate important truths about our interactions with others. I hope it will provide some fresh insights and get you thinking about some things. This is food for thought that tastes good. Like a healthful dessert.

Part 2 deals with communication skills. This part is not meant to be comprehensive or to repeat what is available from other sources, but rather to hit the highlights and focus on the really important parts that often get neglected when one is way into the details. The discussion starts with one-on-one communications, telephone and electronic communication, interviews, then meetings, giving talks, and finally written communications. This ordering generally reflects our impacting increasingly larger numbers of people at a time. We all recognize the importance of one-on-one communications, but some people don't attend many meetings (lucky souls!), give many talks, or write many documents in their work. But remember to think of what you do off the job also. Every time we get together with people or write a note, we're impacting others, and we want to do that effectively.

Part 3 is lagniappe. I heard that term frequently during the time I lived in Louisiana. It means something extra that a merchant throws in, particularly for a good customer. In the vein of the "baker's dozen" that contains 13 items. It's just some extra stuff, some reflections on things I've seen. Some of it relates to interpersonal relationships and skills (and more specifically to motivation), but it's too subtle to fit into Part 1. But it's too good to keep to myself. I hope you enjoy it and find it helpful.

I hope this book will be helpful to people in their work. I've seen how crucial these skills are in the work environment. But I don't want anyone to think that this topic is just for those who work outside the home. We all deal with people every day, and it's important to us that we are effective in doing so. Although the details differ, the basic skills for effective interpersonal relationships and communication are the same for a group of people on a corporate Board of Directors, a work task force, a church or scout troop committee, or a soccer team. The dynamics of a meeting are similar whether its a corporate board meeting, a work group meeting, a community committee meeting, or a PTA meeting. You want to be effective in dealing with your work associates, your friends, your neighbors, and your kids.

I'm convinced that these interpersonal skills and communication skills are the keys to a rewarding professional and personal life. I've seen how they separate the highly successful people from those who just get along. Again, I'm using "successful" in the broadest possible sense here. These skills enable us to accomplish more with our lives and hence obtain more satisfaction.

Let's be clear about our objective. We want to develop skills to be as **effective** as possible in our dealings with others. That is, we want to be able to accomplish our objectives with others. I don't mean being manipulative. We're not just being nice to people because that's a good thing to do (although feel free to be nice if you want to). Our objective is to be effective with others. This practical stuff to help us.

Are interpersonal and communication skills something you're born with? Are some people just better at these things while others are worse, and that's that? No! These are skills that can be developed. You just have to want to improve them, and you have to make this a priority item for you. And if you realize how important they are, you certainly will. So let's get on with it!

PART 1
INTERPERSONAL SKILLS

FOCUS ON OTHERS

Dale Carnegie's book *How to Win Friends and Influence People*[1] is a classic. I highly recommend that you read it if you haven't done so, or re-read it if it's been a while. It defines the basics of interpersonal skills. Vast numbers of people have taken, and I'm sure benefited from, the courses that the Carnegie organization conducts on these principles. The approach is popular because it's successful. In that book you will find suggestions such as:

> Remember and use people's names.
> Be a good listener; encourage others to talk.
> Talk in terms of the other person's interests.
> Make the other person feel important.
> Show honest appreciation and admiration.
> Respect the opinions of others.
> Let the other person do most of the talking.
> Try to see things from the other person's point of view.
> Be sympathetic with the ideas and desires of others.
> Begin with praise and honest appreciation.
> Ask questions instead of giving direct orders.
> Let the other person save face.
> Praise every improvement.
> Ask the person to do you a favor that makes him feel important.

What's the common thread in all this? How would you sum up the essence of it?

I can summarize it in just three words:

FOCUS ON OTHERS (FOO) — Key 1

If you learn nothing else from what I've written here, I hope you'll remember, and use, that key to effective interpersonal skills. Always focus on others! We need to constantly strive to think about what the other person is thinking and feeling and the reason why, and we need to let that knowledge guide our thoughts, words, and actions. That's the key not only to helping him and being nice to him, but also to accomplishing what we want. FOO!

In a youth group with which I worked, an election was held for the top office. Each of the six boys running for it were given an opportunity to say a few words on their behalf just prior to the election. Five of them told about their qualifications for the office. The sixth boy told about how the organization would be better because of what he would do if elected. He focused on the audience and what they would get out of this, rather than on himself. Good idea?

In the movie *City of Angels*, Maggie is eating a pear when Seth asks, "What does that taste like?" She replies, "Don't you know what a pear tastes like?" He then replies, "I don't know what a pear tastes like to you."

Can we develop the skill to really see and experience things as someone else does?

Remember that the entire universe, with one very tiny exception, is composed of others.

Don is one of my past supervisors, and one I've most enjoyed working with. We were discussing a new supervision course that the company had developed and that we'd be taking. He said, "I already know how to be better than I am."

In many respects, including interpersonal relationships, we all probably already know how to be better than we are. We just need to remind ourselves of the importance of focusing on others and be aware of little things we can do every day to improve.

SELF-ESTEEM

The first step to focusing on others, and hence to improving our interpersonal skills, is to:

RECOGNIZE THE EXTREME IMPORTANCE OF SELF-ESTEEM (THE OTHER PERSON'S!) — Key 2

We need to understand how extremely important it is for the other person to find ways to feel good about himself. Most of us go to great lengths to find ways to feel good about ourselves. A person can take just about any setback or criticism so long as he can save face, perhaps finding a rationale so that he can continue to feel that he's a valuable being. We need to keep that foremost in our minds and constantly seek ways to help the other person continue to feel good about himself.

A person's view of himself is the key to his or her success and happiness.

Shad Helmstetter[2] tells how as a boy he longed to play a musical instrument and be a member of a school band. At age twelve he finally got his chance to try out for the school band. He knew his tryout hadn't gone too well, but then he accidentally overheard the band director comment to an associate, "That boy has absolutely no musical ability; he'll never play any instrument decently." For many years he avoided trying to play any instrument. As an adult, he finally got up the courage to rent a piano and started practicing on his own when no one was around to remind him that he couldn't play. He was amazed to find that he could learn to play the piano, and he became quite competent at it. For over twenty frustrating years he had avoided musical instruments because of what he heard the band director say. And the band director was wrong!

In his book *What to Say When You Talk to Yourself*[2], Helmstetter discusses the prevalence of that kind of negative programming. He says that we must re-program ourselves to keep flooding ourselves with messages about what we can do (not what we can't do).

Karl Wallenda, the high-wire artist, fell to his death in 1978 while traversing a high wire in Puerto Rico. Afterwards, his wife, also an aerialist, told how for three months prior to the fall Karl kept thinking and talking about falling. It was the first time he'd done that. He seemed to be focusing on not falling rather than on walking the tightrope. He personally supervised the installation of that tightrope to be sure it was secure, something he'd never even thought of doing before. All that focus on *not* falling seemed to lead to his fall.

If negative thinking and self-doubt can be so harmful, surely a positive view of one's self can be very powerful.

I'm the second child in my family. Thus I can relate to all that you hear about the struggles of the second child to live up to the expectations set by the first child. I don't think it bothered me as a kid, but I think about it now. I was amused by an article that Erma Bombeck wrote about the second child. She said that he will either be the president of a bank, or he will rob one. Yes, we're all going to get our feeling of importance (self worth) one way or another, regardless of our birth order. The challenge is for us to get that feeling of importance in ways that are acceptable to our society. We also need to do it in ways that do not interfere with the functioning of ourselves and others.

4

I'm sure you've noticed how it's usually the person who's not so sure of himself who acts like a bully, tyrant, or show-off.

Having a healthy self-esteem means appreciating our own worth as a person, with certain strengths and weaknesses, and feeling very valuable. It is not egotism. We're all good at some things and not so good at others. We're all smart, just in different ways. Similarly, we're all ignorant, just in different ways. Thank goodness we're all different. We can complement each other.

Sometimes it seems like our self-esteem is like a piece of furniture with good wood, like oak, underneath, but a veneer of cheap, soft wood on the outside. At times it doesn't take much to damage the veneer. Maybe a cutting remark, a snub, a new situation we're not comfortable with, a difficult and strange task to do. We think: "I'm losing it," "I'm not sure I can do this," or "What if I blow this one?". But then we come to the oak underneath and we regain control, thinking: "I can do this; it's not so different from other things I've done; relax." The good experiences we've had form a foundation that keeps us going.

I enjoy both water skiing and snow skiing. I can't say which I enjoy more or which is harder, but I can say that snow skiing is scarier. When snow skiing, you can control your speed by zigzagging across the slope. The problem is that whenever you turn, your skis point directly down the mountain for a moment and you gain speed quickly. If something gets in your way or you falter a bit, causing you to point down the mountain for longer than you had intended, you can easily get going faster than you feel comfortable with. It's easy to get tripped up by a bump and lose your balance, particularly on a turn. One thing I discovered early in my snow-skiing experience is that when that happens if I think to myself, "Oh no, I'm going to fall," then I will. It's as though that thought causes my body to give up, and down I go. A self-fulfilling prophecy. On the other hand, if I say determinedly to myself, "I'm not going to fall; I can recover from this," then I will. Having confidence is the key to success. And you don't have to be great at something to have confidence (witness my skiing). You just need that "can do" attitude. Confidence comes in *cans*. "I can do this."

When watching a track meet, did you ever wonder what the high jumper or pole-vaulter is doing as he stands at the beginning of the runway about to start his jump? He's doing more than just thinking about the jump. He's visualizing himself going up and over that bar, watching how each part of his body moves perfectly. In this visualization, he doesn't see himself hitting the bar. If he thinks that will happen then it probably will. No, he visualizes the successful jump, seeing each arm and leg move into perfect position above the bar. Divers and gymnasts too, just before they start, visualize themselves doing a perfect performance. Believing it can happen makes it a possibility.

Self-confidence is one element in a positive self-esteem. The other part is valuing ourself as a unique person making valuable contributions to the world.

I hope what I've said so far doesn't get us focusing too much on just our own individual self-esteem. We need to be aware and sensitive to the self-esteem of others also. When we encounter a stranger somewhere, we have no idea what's been going on in his or her life. We don't know if he's been through some experiences that have pushed his self-esteem near rock bottom. People have problems, and they don't advertise them. We all accumulate some baggage as we move through our lives and operate within certain constraints. Even with people we know, or think we know, there are important things about them we don't know. Things aren't always as they seem. If we make a rude or cutting comment or snub that person, that may be just enough to push him over the edge into big trouble. Of course, we might never even know about the suffering, but we surely wouldn't want to contribute to it.

The fraternity I joined in college uses a little essay titled "The True Gentleman." The pledges memorize it, and hopefully they and the actives think about it from time to time. A major point of it is the idea of not making others conscious of their weaknesses, limitations, or problems, keeping in mind the other person's self-esteem and our possible impact on it.

Dale Carnegie[3] says, "Almost every man you meet feels himself superior to you in some way; and a sure way to his heart is to let him realize . . . that you recognize his importance." Whether you admit it or not, everyone is superior to you in some way, just as you're superior to him in other ways. We're all different because of the different experiences we've had so far in life. We all have some strengths and some weaknesses, some things we're good at and some things we're not so good at, some things we know a lot about and some things we know little or nothing about. We need to capitalize on this diversity to get things done most effectively and take full advantage of everyone's abilities. The process starts with recognizing those abilities and enabling others to reach their full potential because they're positive about that potential.

THE POWER OF EXPECTATIONS

The second step in focusing on others is to recognize the importance of our expectations on the behavior and performance of others. When we expect them to do great things, and let them know that, then that's just what they do. When we expect problems, we get them.

The high schools in our area have girls' drill teams that perform dance routines as part of the half-time shows at the football games. Our local high school always has an outstanding drill team, called the Silverados, and I've had ample opportunity to observe them through two of my sons who've played in the band. The Silverados sit next to the band. Sonia has directed the Silverados for as many years as I've watched them, and she's obviously very good at what she does. I've made two observations about Sonia. First, she always dresses nicely and looks sharp at the football games. It makes sense that if she wants the girls to look sharp, she should set an example herself. Second, she always addresses this group of high school girls as "ladies." Sonia shows her expectations for the group by the way she looks and speaks.

The phenomenon of expectations becoming reality is called the "Pygmalion effect." In Greek mythology, Pygmalion was a sculptor. He wanted to create a statue of the most beautiful woman imaginable. He worked painstakingly to create this exquisitely beautiful, ivory statue. When completed, she was so beautiful that he fell in love with her and became obsessed with her. In answer to his prayer, the goddess Aphrodite turned the statue into a living woman named Galatea. Pygmalion married Galatea, and they had a son, Paphos.

Pygmalion expected the statue to be beautiful, and it was. The Pygmalion effect refers to the fact that things tend to turn out as we expect them to be. This is not merely a statement of good fortune. It means that our expectations cause things to work out that way. It's a self-fulfilling prophecy.

The story of Pygmalion was the basis for George Bernard Shaw's play "Pygmalion", which in turn gave rise to the musical play and movie *My Fair Lady*. Professor Henry Higgins accepts a challenge from a friend, betting that he can take a poor, common flower girl and, by working on her grammar, poise, dress, etc., fools people into believing she is a woman of royalty. He works steadily to transform this wretch from the bottom rung of society's ladder so that she looks, sounds, and acts like a beautiful, educated woman at the top of that ladder. He pulls off the deception, fooling the royalty at the most elegant social functions. But then, like Pygmalion, he falls in love with this beautiful woman he has created. She had become the true lady that he had expected her to become. Expectation had become reality.

Psychologists have done experiments on the Pygmalion effect, and I saw a movie about their findings. It's amazing! They took a group of students and divided them randomly into two groups. Thus, the two groups did not differ in academic ability or attitude, but they told the teacher of one group that this was a group of gifted students to be challenged to the utmost. They told the teacher of the other group that this was a group of slow learners and behavior problems. The classes met for a year. At the end of the year, the students in the "gifted" class were way ahead of the usual curriculum pace and were enjoying the learning experience immensely. The students in the "slow" class were way behind in the curriculum, bored, and hating school. No difference at the beginning of the year, but such a big difference at the end of the year? Why? Think about it. The teacher of the "gifted" class let those students know he expected high performance from them, heaped all sorts of extra work on them, trusted them, admired them, and gave them so much positive feedback they just soared with him academically. On the other hand, the teacher of the "slow" class let those students know, in subtle ways, that he didn't expect much from them. They would all just do the best they could and make it through the year. Nothing extra, just the basics. He felt he had to watch them carefully or they'd slack off or do something they shouldn't. The students gave him what he expected. Scary? You bet.

In another experiment, they took a group of factory workers and arbitrarily divided them into two groups. Again, no differences in the abilities or attitudes of the two groups. They told the supervisor of one group that his group contained the top performers. They told the supervisor of the other group that he had the bottom of the barrel, the low performance, problem employees who were just short of being fired. The supervisors managed their groups for a year. At the end of that time, those in the "top" group were highly motivated, setting production records, and loving their work. The "bottom" group were disgruntled, doing as little work as they could get by with, and griping endlessly. No difference when they started, but like day and night now. Why? You can imagine how the "lucky" supervisor treated his group of "high performers." He praised them, let them know they were the best and hence he expected the most from them, gave them lots of freedom, and let them run the show to the extent possible. They thrived on it. You can also imagine how the "unlucky" supervisor felt about his crew and how he treated them. He watched them like a hawk, looked for problems, criticized and belittled them, and treated them like children or slaves. They responded accordingly. Scary? You bet.

Jane was a third grade teacher in Iowa who taught her class a lesson about discrimination. But I want to focus on the sub-lesson that was taught on expectations, self-fulfilling prophecies, or the Pygmalion effect. Jane's experiment was reported in a national news broadcast. She divided her class into two groups—the kids with blue eyes and those with brown eyes. She put cloth collars on the brown-eyed kids so they'd be easy to recognize. She told the class that blue-eyed people were smarter, better behaved, did more, and were just generally better than brown-eyed people. Of course, at first the kids didn't believe that, but she quickly convinced them with a few examples. She continued schoolwork during this exercise, and she pointed out when a blue-eyed kid would do something well and when a brown-eyed kid would make a mistake, forget something, and so on. She generalized about how that's just the way blue-eyed or brown-eyed people are. She kept the two groups separate in the classroom, told them not to associate with the other group, and had some different rules for the groups that were designed to make the brown-eyed group feel inferior.

The class regularly worked with a set of flash cards and were timed on how quickly they completed the set of cards. On this day, the blue-eyed kids completed the cards in record time, showing amazing spirit. The brown-eyed kids took considerably longer than the normal time for the whole class, and were noticeably lethargic.

The next morning Jane told the class she had made a mistake. It was the brown-eyed people who were smarter, better behaved, etc., than the blue-eyed people. She switched the collars to the blue-eyed kids, much to the delight of the brown-eyed kids. The rules were switched. At first the kids were a bit confused, but it didn't take long to demonstrate the truth of her claim with examples of brown-eyed kids doing well and blue-eyed kids screwing up.

Here's the amazing part: On the second day, it was the brown-eyed kids who set the speed record on the flash cards, while the blue-eyed kids took forever. A complete reversal! The kids did what they were expected to do. Expectation had become reality.

Of course, at the end of the experiment Jane made sure that the kids understood that the color of one's eyes has nothing to do with how smart or "good" they are.

With the news broadcast, the experiment gained so much publicity that the school decided to track the lives of the kids in this class. They had a class reunion after graduation from high school and watched videos of the experiment.

They found that the members of this class generally "did better" in their careers than the average graduates of this school. Can you think of a reason for that? These kids saw that how well they did in school, such as on the flash cards, didn't depend on something they couldn't do anything about, like the color of their eyes. No, their performance was within their control. They evidently learned to take control of their lives, think positively, and expect a lot from themselves.

In case you think this is just something to help kids, Jane no longer teaches school but now runs adult classes using the same type of experiment.

Remember when you were in high school? When they'd give a test, some teachers would pace up and down the aisles glaring at you as if to say, "I know you're trying to cheat on this test and I'm going to catch you." It was distracting and annoying. Maybe you'd never given the slightest thought to cheating. But sometimes a strange thought would cross your mind. If she's so sure I'm going to cheat, maybe I should. It would be a challenge to avoid getting caught when that old biddy is so intent on catching me. On the other hand, some teachers would pass out the tests and leave the room to do something else. They trusted you. Now how could you ever cheat on someone who trusted you that much? No, you'd rather make a poor grade than do that. The teacher's expectation influenced your actions.

On a route that I traveled a number of times there was a small motel I used to stay at because it was at a convenient stopping point. I traveled off the expressway into the town to reach it. It was cheaper than the motels right on the expressway. It was right beside a railroad track, a fact that I discovered during the middle of the first night I stayed there. When I ate in their restaurant and stopped at the counter on my way out to pay my bill, there was no one at that counter. An assortment of money was spread out on the counter. They expected a person to just pay and make his own change. The honor system. Now who could cheat a place that was that trusting? Their expectations were fulfilled.

I think the Pygmalion effect works largely because people's self-esteem is affected by the expectations we show them. They may not even realize they're being affected by us.

THE WAY PEOPLE ACT DEPENDS ON HOW WE EXPECT THEM TO ACT. — Key 3

That's scary even if you're not a teacher or a boss. What about a parent? We all interact with people every day. Can the way we treat them have that much impact on what they do? You bet. It's scary, but it's wonderful too.

Be careful of what you expect of others, because that's what you'll get.

If you want to get people to do more, raise your expectations.

Each of us carries a great responsibility for how we treat others. Each of us can have a great influence on how others act. That's real power. Let's strive to use it wisely.

UNDERSTANDING OTHERS

The commuter train was heading into the city early one morning. Some of the riders were catching a nap; others were reading the paper or a book. It was very quiet. Then a man boarded the train with three young children. The quiet ended. The kids were running around the train car constantly chattering. The man just sat there sort of staring into space seemingly unaware of what his kids were doing. The longer it went on the more it annoyed the other passengers. Their restful ride had been destroyed and this guy couldn't care less. He didn't even notice. Finally, a man sitting near him said, "Do you think you could do something to quiet your kids down? It's very disturbing."

The man appeared a bit startled. He replied, "Oh, yes, I'm sorry. I should do something with them. I guess they're in as bad a shape as I am. It's been rough on them. Their mother passed away this morning."

The riders were shocked. They had no idea. Their mood suddenly changed from anger to compassion, looking for any way they might help this troubled family.4

You see, now they had the correct picture. At first they saw an inconsiderate man with his unruly kids. Their feelings and actions were based on that picture. When they got the correct picture, the resulting feelings and actions were much different. We need to watch out for incorrect views like that.

INSTEAD OF CRITICIZING OTHERS' BEHAVIOR, TRY TO UNDERSTAND WHY THEY BEHAVE AS THEY DO. — Key 4.

Then it will be clear what you should do about it. This is a crucial aspect of focusing on others.

Why is that co-worker so arrogant and bossy? What experiences has he been through that have led to that attitude? What's he trying to accomplish? Why is that neighbor so cold and aloof? What's she thinking about? Is she that way with everyone, or is it something about me that causes it? Why is my boss so opinionated and closed-minded? Does he think he has to portray that image to get ahead? Do the expectations of *his* boss cause him to act that way? Why is that woman so nervous and defensive? What kind of bad experiences has she had in situations like this? Is she trying to save face? Why is he such a know-it-all? Is it to compensate for something he's not so confident about?

We need to ask a lot of questions. We need to talk with the person, even if that's not the most pleasant experience, and, most importantly, we need to really listen. It takes time and effort, but if we want to be effective with people we must do it. Here's a clue—you'll often find that the behaviors relate to getting that feeling of self worth I discussed earlier.

Even when we expend this extra effort, we don't know what's going on in other people's lives. We don't know what burdens they're carrying. As I've gotten older and seen more of people, I've become more tolerant. Understanding others better makes us more tolerant.

The next three sections further explore aspects of understanding others.

MOTIVATION

A key area in which we need to understand others is *what motivates them*. These are basically the same things that motivate us, because other people are not fundamentally different from us. It's also important to understand the negative side, i.e., what "demotivates" people.

THE ONLY KIND OF MOTIVATION THAT REALLY WORKS AND LASTS
IS SELF-MOTIVATION. — Key 5.

It's also called intrinsic motivation. It's based on values within us related to our self-esteem and the joy and pride we feel in what we do. We can pick up some useful tips from a motivational speaker or a motivational book. We may come away from such things fired up, for a while. But motivation given by someone else has a limited effect and is only temporary. Effective, lasting motivation must come from within.

Think about the great athletes, like Olympic champions. They're not motivated by their coaches or teammates. They're self-motivated. They're dedicated to, and focused on, excellence. They set their own standards, goals, and training programs. That's the only way they can achieve so much. All that drive comes from within!

Professional (career) motivation is the same. If you're motivated by your boss or by things your employer offers, like salary, impressive titles, perks, power, and big offices, then at some point in your career you're going to lose your motivation. That happens because there are inevitable disappointments in those extrinsic, or external, motivators. At some point, you won't feel that you're getting what you deserve. It may take a while, but eventually it will happen, and if that's all that keeps you going, you'll have a problem. To have a truly rewarding career, for your whole career, you have to be self-motivated. You have to strive for excellence in your work because that's what *you* want to do. You have to find your own rewards. Then, in effect, you're your own boss, no matter who you work for. And that's the way it should be for a true professional.

I'm not saying you should be a rebel. Your objectives can, and should, mesh very well with your employer's objectives. You should strive to maximize your value to your employer. But the motivation comes from within you!

Employee motivation is the key to high productivity. If our companies are to be as productive as they need to be to compete well in today's economy, their employees must be highly productive individuals, and that means they must be highly motivated.

All employers strive to hire the most motivated, hard-driving employees they can find. They won't hire someone who lacks drive and ambition. But drive isn't something you learn once and then you've got it, like riding a bike. It's an attitude built up by daily experience in every day of our lives. It can increase or decrease with time, based on the experiences we go through. It's determined by the cumulative effects of all our interactions with others.

We need to find ways to keep our employees highly motivated, and that means we need to take a hard look at why many employees become "demotivated" at some point in their careers. Think about the common pattern. We go to great lengths to hire the best employees we possibly can. They join us all fired up to do great things. They dig in and work hard in those early years. But those ambitious young employees are a sharp contrast to many of our older employees. The latter are cynical, negative, apathetic, perhaps coasting until retirement when they should be making such great contributions because of all their experience. They have just as much talent as the young go-getters, and they used to be go-getters themselves, but something has changed. It's tragic! We need to find out what has changed and put a stop to it, because it's killing our companies.

Before I go on let me emphasize that I said *many of our older employees.* It's important to know that not all employees suffer this problem. It's not an inevitable consequence of aging or experience. Some employees remain highly motivated until they retire, which is as it should be (You can bet these folks are also highly motivated after they retire, just toward different objectives.) The fact that not all employees become "demotivated" gives us hope, and may provide clues for solving, or at least lessening, this problem.

Let's think about that young go-getter. He's fired up because he believes that he has the talent to do good work and that he'll be rewarded appropriately for that work as his career progresses. He chose an employer that he believes values the kind of contributions he can make. He hits the ground running. What could possibly cause that employee to lose his motivation as his career progresses? Let me suggest some possibilities.

1. Bosses who are jerks.

New employees tend to be somewhat in awe of their bosses. They don't know how the boss got there or much about him, but they treat him with respect. However, the recent hire may soon find out that his boss doesn't know much about—or have much appreciation for—the work he's doing. He may start to wonder what's really important to his boss, and this relates to performance appraisal, since this boss is the individual having the most input in evaluating his performance. He may wonder what criteria the boss measures him against. Is he rated on how much he's like his boss?

A favorite is when the go-getter works his tail off and puts in lots of overtime to get a piece of work done on time, only to have his boss sit on it for a week before finding a chance to give it his superficial half-hour review. And it's even worse if the boss still finds time for two-hour lunches and lots of chitchat while the work is sitting. He thinks, "If it's O.K. for work to be a week late, next time I'll take it easier and use the extra week."

2. Promotion policies.

When the new hire joins the company, he looks around and sees the various people in their various positions, and everything appears logical. The managers at various levels seem to fit their positions. He presumes that there are good reasons why they're all where they are. But as the years go by, he sees people change positions and he begins to see some younger people moving into leadership positions. At times he wonders why employee A was promoted rather than employee B, who seems to be contributing more. He wonders what the criteria for promotion are. Maybe he wonders about criteria for "demotion" too. And he wonders what this means for his own chances for promotion. Maybe he's emphasizing the wrong things as far as getting ahead goes.

3. Unchallenging work.

Before long, the recent hire finds himself doing tasks that are much less than he's capable of. Maybe it's because support people have been cut to reduce costs. Maybe the company has such a bare-bones staff that they contract out all the good work and just expect their employees to be contract monitors. He wonders, "Is this what I spent all those years in college (or training) for?"

4. Time wasters.

The go-getter is working his tail off, putting in overtime and striving hard to be as efficient as possible because there's so much to do. But he soon finds that he has to attend certain worthless meetings and take care of mindless bureaucratic nonsense and "administrivia." He asks himself, "Why should I bust my butt trying to do all this work when the company makes me waste time on junk like this? If they don't care whether I get any worthwhile work done or not, why should I care?"

5. Pigeonholing.

Although he was hired for his strong and unique abilities, he finds there are some who think he should be like everyone else. They seem to want all their employees to be interchangeable so they can be moved around like pawns on a chessboard. His unique abilities are not appreciated.

There are some obvious relationships among these items. I'm sure you can think of more, similar items.

I made some overseas trips with a man who was close to retirement. I was impressed with how aggressively he'd attack technical problems while on those trips. He just loved getting into a tough problem and solving it. We worked up a solution to one problem, but when we presented it to others in an afternoon meeting we realized that we had missed the boat. The next morning we had to give another, higher-level presentation on the same topic. We worked together before and after dinner to correct what we'd done. At about eleven P.M. I gave him the last of my part. The rest was work he'd done and that he'd have to correct. I went to bed. The next morning I learned that he had stayed up all night working on it. He was dedicated! We gave the presentation, which went fine, then he went back to the hotel to sleep. Such was the way he worked when he was five thousand miles from the office.

But in the office he was a completely different man. He was bitter, cynical, derogatory, uncooperative, unmotivated, and unproductive—like a different person. Why? A few conversations with him made it clear. He'd been in positions of high responsibility, but now had little. His boss treated him like a new-hire. He didn't feel appreciated. He hated all the bureaucracy and time-wasting at the office. When he was off on a trip, he left all that behind. There he was in charge and there was nothing to hold him back.

A night-versus-day difference in performance, due to a night-versus-day difference in motivation due to a difference in working environment. How tragic when we create an environment that destroys motivation and productivity! And how stupid and unnecessary!

How can we summarize? The go-getter can become "demotivated" by things he sees or experiences over the years, things that change his view of the corporate culture. Is this new picture a necessary correction of a naive, unrealistic view? I don't think so. His initial vision of the company culture was the one we sold him on, and since we weren't deliberately deceptive, we must believe that the culture he envisioned is the one we really want to exist. We want our company to be one in which people focus on the work our customers want, and one in which they are appreciated and rewarded accordingly. We know that in order for our company to compete effectively we must make the best use of the great talent that our people have. So how do we stop the "demotivation?" By getting our priorities back to the way we really want them to be.

This isn't just a big company matter. The situation is the same whether you have three employees or thousands of them. Motivation (and avoiding "demotivation") involves one-on-one interactions, so numbers aren't important. In your personal life, it might just be between you and one other person.

I want to relate a few true stories about "demotivation." They're of a negative nature, but we can learn from negative examples as well as positive ones.

Les had over twenty years experience with the company and was the computer guru of the accounting department. He was responsible for keeping the mainframe accounting programs running. He knew how essential those programs are for the daily work, so when he'd get a call at home in the middle of the night or on a weekend he'd go into the office and fix the problem at once, no matter how long it took. Even though he wasn't paid overtime for such work, his company had a policy that employees were reimbursed for mileage and any meals associated with having to come to work at times off the regular schedule. Ever since that policy had been implemented, Les had turned in expense accounts accordingly and had been reimbursed. But then he got a new supervisor, and she wouldn't approve such expenses so Les stopped making the special trips to fix the system. He'd just take care of it the next time he was in the office. There wasn't much money involved; it was the principle that bothered him. If it wasn't worth the expense reimbursement, then it wasn't worth disrupting his life for, either. The others in his department were upset that they couldn't do their work because the system was down, but they knew who was to blame. Some might ask why he didn't fight it, since he was acting in accordance with company policy, but some employees figure it doesn't pay to fight management. Such a little thing, and even one that was wrong, ruined the internal motivation of a dedicated employee:

A boss came into a room where two secretaries were preparing a set of notebooks for him for an upcoming meeting. They were busily inserting pages into the notebooks. He said, "I hope you're getting that stuff in there in the right place." One of the secretaries later related that she felt insulted. She casually mentioned it to the boss's secretary. The boss's secretary said, "Oh, he does that to me all the time. I'll be doing something at my desk and he'll say, 'I hope you're doing that right.' I usually look him in the eye and say, 'No, I'm doing it wrong.'"

In spite of such hints from his secretary, he keeps giving people the message that he doesn't trust them and expects them to screw up. He just doesn't get it.

A new production facility was being built. As usually happens, the company set a date by which the first production was to be accomplished, and everyone started working toward that date. A number of delays occurred, but no one wanted to give up on the target startup date, so the employees just pushed harder and harder. The closer the date came, the more difficult it became to accomplish it. Then a big boss in the company announced that he would be at the new facility on the startup day to celebrate the accomplishment. That really put the pressure on the employees. Their workdays days got longer and longer, and they were wearing down, but the thought of reaching that difficult goal and showing the boss they could do it kept them going.

Finally, the big startup day arrived, and almost miraculously, they did get the facility started up and made their first production that day, shortly before the boss arrived. Many of the employees had slept only four or five hours a night for the past week, and many had been up all night that last night. They were exhausted but exhilarated by their great accomplishment, like an athlete after a big win. They dragged their weary bodies out to the entrance to meet the boss, anxious to hear his reaction to the accomplishment. The boss arrived, looked around, saw some materials lying around from the work that had been going on, and said, "This place is a mess! Why don't you clean it up?"

Some time later that boss was transferred to another location. The employees at that facility literally danced in the streets!

Motivation or "demotivation?" Do we think about our impact on our co-workers? Do we focus on others as much as we should to achieve the best performance?

A person's self-motivation is the key to his or her success. I've seen so many people who have everything they need to be successful except one thing, drive, which means self-motivation. But without that one thing, the person is headed for mediocrity. Fortunately, we control our self-motivation.

A person's self-motivation can be the result of any number of experiences he or she has had. Let me illustrate the possibilities with a true story:

A man who was very successful in his field was asked, "What incident in your life most contributed to your success?" He replied that it was an incident that occurred about forty years earlier. He was working in his study while also trying to keep an eye on a group of kids playing outside his window. His son, who was then five years old, was among the kids. When the kids became unusually quiet, he wondered what they were up to. From his window, he saw that they were seated in a group. He listened in a bit, and heard them discussing what they wanted to be when they grew up. One boy said he wanted to be a train engineer so he could blow the train whistle. Another wanted to be a fireman so he could slide down the pole and steer the back end of the long fire truck. Other kids chimed in with similar items of interest to youngsters. But then his son said, "I want to be a man just like my dad." It stunned him. Six months later the boy died. The man said that he spent the rest of his life striving to be the kind of man that his boy wanted to grow into.

ATTITUDES

What is the context in which we hear the most about attitudes? We hear about someone having a "bad attitude". Someone asked a young boy an innocuous question about his attitude, and he replied "My teacher says mine's bad." Does that mean maybe it's defective? We talk of "attitude adjustment" (to change it). We refer to something as "a _____ with an attitude" (meaning a bad one). So much of what we hear about attitudes is negative. Sure, there are negative attitudes, i.e., attitudes that hold us back. But there are also positive attitudes, i.e., attitudes that spur us on to greater achievement. We hear about someone having a "positive attitude" or a "can-do attitude." But we don't hear enough about such attitudes.

There's a little plaque hanging in our house bearing this quotation:

"Keep your face to the sunshine and you cannot see the shadow."—Helen Keller

Think about it physically—you don't see shadows when you're facing the sun. Think about it philosophically. When you look on the bright side you don't see the dark side. Then think about the fact that this was written by a blind woman.

A positive attitude means avoiding the "donut-hole mentality," focusing on what's missing rather than what's there.

A positive attitude is closely related to an open mind. Consider this:

"Common sense is nothing more than a deposit of prejudices laid down in the mind prior to the age of eighteen."

— Albert Einstein

I find this interesting because some of Einstein's brilliant work caused us to set aside some ideas that were so firmly entrenched they could have been considered common sense. His Theory of Relativity showed a variation of time previously unimagined, and his work on nuclear energy showed that matter is not always conserved.

A positive attitude toward our self is also important, and this obviously relates to the matter of self-esteem discussed earlier.

Optimism is a positive attitude, and it's a habit of thinking. A study by the Mayo Clinic indicated that optimistic people live longer.

The yearbook produced each year at my high school was very good. Many years it won awards. Each yearbook had a theme that was carried throughout the book. My senior year the theme was "Enthusiasm, The Priceless Ingredient." Maybe it's just because that was the theme, but it seemed like the enthusiasm could be seen on the faces of students in so many pictures in that yearbook. I particularly remember the face of the catcher on our baseball team, looking out through his mask with marked enthusiasm and the face of a girl square dancing, coming under a couple's upraised arms. The book included Emerson's quotation, "Nothing great was ever accomplished without enthusiasm." Enthusiasm is an attitude. Sometimes we say that someone has "infectious enthusiasm." Enthusiasm is infectious.

I like the bumper sticker that says, "Courtesy is contagious. Let's start an epidemic." Courtesy is an attitude.

All attitudes, both positive and negative, are infectious or contagious. They're passed from one person to those around him. One person can pull a whole group up or down with his or her attitude. We need to be alert to what we and others are passing around, and to control it.

KEEP A POSITIVE AND ENTHUSIASTIC ATTITUDE, AND PASS IT ON TO EVERYONE YOU CAN. — Key 6

"Attitude is the paintbrush of the mind. It colors everything."

MOTIVATION AND ATTITUDES ABOUT WORK

Motivation and attitudes are crucial to our effectiveness and satisfaction in all aspects of our lives. But I want to focus a bit on our motivation for—and our attitudes toward—our work, i.e., the work we get paid for. This is important because it affects the productivity of our commercial organizations and, on a larger scale, even our nation's economy. If our companies, and our nation, are to be competitive in today's global economy, we must have highly productive employees, and a person's productivity on the job depends on his or her motivation and attitudes toward that job.

Work is a privilege. We can't do it when we're too young; we're striving to get the education and maturity we'll need to work later. We can't do it when we're too old, although this end is fuzzier. Most older folks stop working at some point because of employer age limits, health problems, or because it's no longer financially necessary. (By the way, I hear that we're now supposed to refer to the elderly as the "chronologically gifted"). Some unfortunate people can't work at all. The majority of us, who get to work that middle part of our lives, should savor those years.

I appreciate humor, and I hope people are only joking when they adorn their vehicles with bumper stickers saying, "I owe, I owe, so off to work I go" or "A bad day fishing is better than a good day at work." Sure, most of us need to work to support ourselves and our families, but I feel sorry for anyone who feels that he works only for the money. Sure, we all enjoy recreation. But I feel sorry for anyone who really doesn't like his or her job.

Think about the organizations we work for, from the largest to the smallest. Those organizations exist to provide goods and services people need or want. In other words, to make life a bit more pleasant for all of us. That may include some excesses for the rich, and no one has much empathy for them, but it also includes things that make life more enjoyable for "average" folks, and things to reduce the suffering of people who have real problems of many types.

As we do the work of these organizations, we're doing our part to help others, make life more pleasant, and make the world a better place. When you look at the "big picture," you see how important our work is. We can do some good with some of the money we earn. Our work is a creative outlet, an opportunity to express ourselves. I know some people's jobs don't seem so much that way, but there's something to the way we think about and approach our jobs.

A man approached a construction site and asked one of the workmen what he was doing. He said, "I'm pouring concrete."

He went a bit further and asked another man. This one said, "I'm building up this face of the steeple."

He went on and asked the same question of a third worker. He replied, "I'm building a magnificent church in which people will worship for many, many years." They were all physically doing the same thing—pouring concrete, but what vastly different views of their work they had. I'm sure it made a big difference in the way the felt about getting up every morning to go to that job, and how they felt when they arrived home at the end of the day. There's nothing foolish about seeing the big picture.

All jobs have a creative aspect, and that can be the key to

enjoying them more. We all like to be creative. Like when we bake a cake, for example. Now I know a few very creative people bake cakes from scratch, but most of us prefer using cake mixes. Even I can do it, and my cooking skills are limited. I just follow the directions. Pour the mix into a bowl, add the eggs and water, mix, put in the baking pan, and bake. A cinch. All the ingredients are in the mix. You add water, not milk, because they include powdered milk in the mix. Why don't they include powdered eggs in the mix too, so you can just add water and nothing else? Manufacturers tried it in the first cake mixes and found that people didn't want to just add water. It wasn't creative enough. Cracking a couple of eggs into the bowl added just the element of creativity people wanted. And most jobs we're employed for involve a lot more creativity than cracking eggs.

I'm sure some of you are old enough to remember the "Jiggs" cartoons. Jiggs' wife was Maggie. Jiggs was feeling bad one morning, having a hard time getting out of bed, so he told Maggie, "I think I'll stay home today and rest."

She replied, "Oh, Jiggs, don't baby yourself like that. You get up and go to work and you'll feel fine."

So Jiggs dragged himself off to work. The next frame shows him at his desk, feet up, leaning back, sound asleep. When he gets home Maggie says, "See, don't you feel better since you went to work?"

He says, "I sure do!"

There are some mornings we don't feel like going to work. Sometimes we're ill enough that we shouldn't go to work. I err on the "carry them to work on a stretcher" side, but I certainly feel sorry for anyone who doesn't feel like going to work because there's nothing there to look forward to.

I know it sounds corny, but I love my work. I look forward to going each morning. I sometimes find myself hurrying to get there, taking the stairs two at a time, because I'm anxious to get started. I often work through lunch. A few times I've awakened during the night thinking about a good way to do something, and lay there working out some of the details. Am I crazy? I don't think so. Am I a workaholic? I don't think so. I have other interests and don't work excessive hours. The work is interesting, challenging, important, and I enjoy doing it. The people I work with are highly competent and very pleasant, that's all. I'm not alone in this.

John works where I do. The first few years I worked there we worked in the same group. He's a real whiz at math and computers. People go to see him when they have a really tough problem. He considers math and computers his hobby also. He said that he's in a fortunate situation in that he gets paid for doing his hobby.

We all know about Bill Gates, the chief founder of Microsoft. He founded the company when he was only nineteen years old. As a result of his success with Microsoft, he was a billionaire by the time he was thirty one years old and is now one of the richest people in the world. Of course, with all that money he could live in style without working. Being the top dog at his company, he could delegate everything and direct it all with as little effort as he desired to contribute. But he still works 75 hours per week like he used to. He still sometimes wakes up in the middle of the night with an idea and stays up most of the night working out the details. He says about his work: "This is fun stuff." "We're designing cool things here, and when it works, I still get very excited." He says he'd like to be younger, so he could stay up two nights in a row, like he used to. Is he eccentric or a nut? I doubt it. I think he's just a guy who loves his work, his company, and what it's doing. Wonderful!

The President of the United States earns $400,000 per year. That's a lot of money, but it's a tremendous job that has taken a heavy toll on many who have held it. Have you compared some of the before-and-after pictures of past presidents? Most of the men who have held that job in recent years were wealthy enough before they took it that they certainly didn't do it for the money, although some may have been hungry for power and fame. However, the primary motivation is probably the chance to make a major contribution to the world, to make a difference.

My father taught me some things about work without saying a word about it. He was in the car and truck rental business. He worked for a fairly large firm, then in partnership with two others, with each of them operating his own branch. Near the end of his career, he went back to employment by a company. In this case he operated a car rental business at a car dealership. In the morning, customers would line up in their cars outside the service door waiting for the business to open at 7 A.M. Dad and the service personnel were there before 7 A.M. He asked the service people, "Why don't you open the door and get an early start?"

They said, "Not until 7 A.M.."

He said, "Can't you at least let them pull their cars in out of the cold to wait?"

Again, "Not until 7 A.M.." Having operated a business of his own, he found this attitude hard to believe. That wasn't the way he viewed his work, his way of meeting customers needs, his contribution to the world.

When we just do what's required of us, we're slaves. When we go beyond that to do the extra, optional things, then we become free.

A man related something he saw on an airplane flight: It was a Continental flight, and he was sitting up in the first-class section. He noticed that a man sitting in front of him, while looking around the plane, spotted a little dirt smudge above him. He reached up with a napkin and wiped it off. That man was Gordon Bethune, the CEO of Continental Airlines. He saw a little thing that needed improvement, didn't get angry at anyone about it, but just took care of it.

Most people strongly relate work and success. We want to be successful in our work. Of course, people's views of success vary greatly. I don't think success necessarily relates to income or wealth. It relates more to being good at and enjoying what you do. It seems like being good at something and enjoying it is a sort of "chicken and egg" situation, it's not obvious which comes first. We tend to be good at things we enjoy, and to enjoy doing things we're good at. There are some fields of work, such as teaching, in which it's almost impossible to make much money even if you're excellent at it. On the other hand, there are other fields (I'll skip examples here) in which you evidently can make a lot of money even if you're mediocre.

My son wrote an essay in which he stated his belief that *the secret of success is hard work.* His high school cross-country coach helped teach him that. At one sports dinner his coach joked that scientists were working on a pill people could take to become star athletes without having to work at it. I think my son and his former coach are right. There may be some exceptions, but by and large, in the industrial world where I work, the people who are successful work hard. Those who excel in a professional field, in management, or in their own business take their jobs very seriously, work long hours, and work efficiently. They push themselves, handle a lot of stress, and make efforts to keep improving and learning.

I think of the two famous heart surgeons who work in my area—Denton Cooley and Michael DeBaakey—and all those miraculous heart operations and transplants they do. They couldn't possibly reach that level of excellence and accomplishment without a true dedication to their work.

Perfectionism can get in our way if it's misdirected, but there are places where it's just great. I don't know about you, but if I'm going to have heart surgery or brain surgery I want that surgeon to be a perfectionist. He can't be too exacting or nitpicky, as far as I'm concerned. I feel the same way about the pilots on the commercial jets I ride. I hope they won't tolerate anything less than perfection.

When I see one of those big-production musical plays as are so popular in New York and London, I think about the work of the cast. The more successful the show, the longer it runs, and a lot of them run for years. Some actors and actresses have made a name for themselves with just one outstanding role in one of those blockbuster musicals. They play the same role five or six nights a week for years! I know they have stand-ins, or seconds, who give them some breaks and I suppose they might get sick occasionally, but basically they're performing five or six nights a week for years. They do the same thing over and over. Can you imagine doing that? How can they go out on that stage every night with such enthusiasm and give a magnificent performance night after night for so long? Surely they must focus on the fact that, although the performance is the same for them every night, it's a different audience every night. The people in that audience haven't seen the performance before, and this will be their only chance to see it so it has to be great! We consider actors and actresses to be glamorous jobs. We enjoy so much that one great performance we see, but we don't think about all the other performances they must provide.

Sometimes we can tire from the repetition of a job, so we need to focus on the person who benefits from our work. To him, only one of our repetitions has meaning. For him, that shot is everything!

A person's attitude toward his or her work is so important. A positive, "can do" attitude is such a key factor. When I think of positive attitudes, I think of a brilliant man I was privileged to work closely with for a year. His name was Jack. Our task was to provide guidance to a research laboratory in two ways: First, we tried to identify research areas in which some successful work could yield significant benefits for the company. Second, we tried to find practical applications for the "inventions" the laboratory people came up with.

Jack acquainted me with a large number of key contacts throughout the company, people with whom I could "bounce off" new ideas. They were sharp people who knew a lot about various areas, and they certainly strived to be helpful. I soon learned that that it was easy for people to find something wrong with an idea. You know, some reason why it wouldn't work, or would be too expensive, or was like something else that hadn't worked out, or whatever. That's where Jack was different. He could see those things also, but he worked hard to see beyond them. He would ask, "What is the essential problem with the idea? Is there a way to get around that? If it won't work for this, then how about for something else? Is there another problem that needs the 'opposite' type of solution?" And so on. Jack's attitude toward new ideas was what made him so valuable to the company.

Charles Kettering said, "The typical eye sees the ten percent bad of an idea and overlooks the ninety percent good." Jack was by no means typical.

In our society, the worth of a person who works is closely associated with his or her work, which is unfortunate. It means that a setback in one's work is often taken very personally, particularly by the person involved but also by others. Of course, the ultimate setback is losing one's job. I haven't been through that experience, but I'm sure it's hard to look for positive aspects. It's easy to get into the mentality of "woe is me," the poor victim. It's devastating for many people.

I think of Lee Iacocca. He had a very successful career with Ford, working his way up to a high executive level. But then, due to a sort of non-work-related conflict, he was fired. Everything down the tubes. Depressing, I'm sure. But then he took the top job at Chrysler Corporation, pulled that company out of financial difficulties, and became a real hero and public figure. His real success came after he was fired.

I read an item by a "head hunter," a person specializing in matching individuals and positions, particularly for high-level executives. He said that for the really tough positions, such as where a company needs a real turn-around, he looks for someone who has experienced some failures, either in his professional life or his personal life. Obviously, he needs to have some successes also, but the person who has weathered some tough spots seems to have the best insight needed for real accomplishments.

Flexibility is important to job success, and flexibility requires a willingness to, and desire to, keep learning. Bob was a high-performance individual who worked at that research laboratory that I previously mentioned. He told me that he regarded his college education (he had a Ph.D.) as just his first education, and that he'd had many others since. With today's rapidly advancing technology, most of us are working with things we could not have learned about in school because they didn't exist then. A prime example is computers. During my senior year of undergraduate school we used a computer larger than a desk with lots of blinking lights. It read computer cards. It had only a fraction of the computing power of the little PC's now sitting on everyone's desks, and no one has used computer cards for years. In practically every field, the learning never stops. If it does we're done for.

I think of another Bob I worked with who had his work area changed when he was over sixty years old. He had to learn new technology. Most people would have been content to just keep on doing what they were familiar with for a few more years until retirement, just "coast." But Bob was still looking for new challenges. I'll bet he still is.

I remember interviewing Bert for employment at my place of work. When he finished high school he enrolled in college. The first semester he didn't do well, decided college wasn't for him, and quit to take a job with an oilfield company. He worked for them for two years, then for five years as a "roughneck" on an offshore oil platform. A physically tough job. Then he decided he wanted to do something different. He squeezed in some courses at a junior college, then he took a big step: He took the money he had saved, enrolled in college again, and this time went on to obtain a doctorate degree in engineering. As part of his doctoral research he spent a year at a government laboratory working with the top people in his field. I admire Bert for having the guts to make that change, particularly to make another run at college when his first shot at it hadn't been so great. I think he can do about anything he puts his mind to.

Another example of flexibility is the late Edwin Hubble, the famous astronomer. You may have heard of the Hubble telescope that now orbits our earth. Among his major contributions, Hubble demonstrated that there are galaxies beyond the Milky Way, and that the universe is expanding (at a rate described by "Hubble's Law"). He was a brilliant scientist. But he wasn't always a scientist. He studied law and languages in college, then worked a while as a lawyer. How fortunate that he had the insight and courage to make a change, go back to earn his doctorate in astronomy, and then launch a brilliant career.

I also think of Armand Hammer, who died some years ago. He was chairman and chief executive officer of Occidental Petroleum for thirty three years. But before that, between 1931 and 1956, he worked as a merchant banker in Paris, an art dealer in New York City, a cattle breeder in New Jersey, a whiskey distiller in Kentucky, and as the head of the Mutual Broadcasting System. In 1956 he invested in Occidental. That investment led to some successful ventures, and he became CEO the next year. He led the company as it grew to become the seventh largest oil company and the sixteenth largest industrial company in the U.S., with over 53,000 employees. Maybe that great variety of work experiences he had prior to Occidental gave him the background necessary for success.

When I think about attitudes toward work, I think of a man I noticed several times crossing our parking lot before and after work. What was so striking about him was the classy manner in which he dressed. He always wore a suit with all the "trimmings" that looked like something right off the fashion page of a magazine. Really sharp. Then I saw him at work within our building during the day. He looked a lot different, since he was a painter and thus was wearing the usual white overalls that painters wear. Why did he dress up so much just to travel to and from work, when as soon as he got there he had to change into the overalls and wear those all day at work? Most people he saw during the day didn't see his good clothes. I think it had to do with his attitude toward his work. He was a professional; he took his work seriously. His objective was to create neat, good-looking walls, and that objective related to a neat, attractive personal appearance as well.

Our appearance does affect the way we perceive our jobs and the way others perceive us in a professional manner. Think about the last time you flew on a commercial jet. As you boarded the plane, you may have glanced into the cockpit as people often do (I guess to be impressed with all those gauges and switches). What if there in the captain's seat, was a man who evidently was the captain, preparing for the flight, but he wasn't wearing the traditional uniform. This guy looked like he just came off the beach, bare top, cutoffs, sandals, and several days' beard. Would that shake your confidence about the flight? He might be the best pilot around, but somehow you'd probably feel better if he looked like a pilot, right?

I like to see people take pride in their work. Have you seen those ads suggesting that we all sign our work to show we're proud of it? "These windows washed by Henry Jenkins." "This hamburger cooked by Carolyn Evans." Good idea. I've liked it on the few occasions when the little slip of paper in the pocket of a new pair of pants said something like "Inspected by Elizabeth Morgan" rather than "Inspected by No. 62." Maybe I couldn't commend or chastise Elizabeth for her work, but I was glad she told me about it. What really impressed me was a note I found in the box with a toy that required quite a bit of assembly. It gave the name of the man who packed it, stated that he wanted everything to be correct, and gave his home phone number. Now that's a commitment to quality!

Swimming was my big sport when I was a kid. I didn't learn to swim until I was in the seventh grade, but by ninth grade I was really into it. I was on teams in high school, college, and the summers between school years. It was a year-round activity. At a meet during my college years, I was at an "away" meet at Notre Dame. I entered my usual long-distance freestyle events—the 200 and 400 yards. The 400-yard race was near the end of the meet, just before the freestyle relay. I didn't often swim the free relay because it's more for sprinters and it was always just after the 400 free. A quarter mile race, particularly after another race, has a somewhat lasting impact, shall we say. But in this meet I was on the free relay team. I was to swim last on it, not because I was the fastest but so that I'd have a little more time to rest after the 400. Relays are important because a lot of points are awarded for them.

Notre Dame had a good swim team, but it happened that they were a bit weak in long-distance freestyle. The coach thought I could win the 400 easily, so he told me not to swim it any harder than necessary to win. I was to save as much energy as possible for the free relay. Such strategies are common. Well, I won the 400 without trouble, caught my breath, and went all out to help the free relay team.

The Notre Dame team didn't have any good distance swimmers. So some of their swimmers were so impressed with my performance in the 400 that they congratulated me. I was flattered but embarrassed, because it was far from my best time.

But there was even more. It seems Notre Dame had been weak in distance free for some time, and hence their pool record wasn't the greatest. I had set a new pool record with my lackluster performance. They mailed me a fancy certificate stating that I held the pool record. Of course, the certificate had that crummy time on it. Somehow the record and certificate didn't mean too much to me, because it hadn't been my best effort. We always feel a lot better when we've given something our best shot.

My sons and I have discussed the fact that in sports you sometimes win a big, impressive trophy that really doesn't mean much to you because it didn't represent much of an accomplishment. Somewhere in our stashes, I have some old swimming trophies like that. In contrast, sometimes for a really tough competition and a really great effort you just receive a medal, or just a ribbon, that doesn't look that great but that means a great deal to you because of what it represents. The Olympic winners don't get a trophy, just a medal, but think what that medal means. When we look through the spoils of our endeavors, we know which items really mean something and which are just fluff.

In recent years we've been seeing more writing about excellence, quality circles, continuous improvement, etc. Some of that is fed by concerns about keeping up in increasingly intense worldwide industrial competition. There's nothing mysterious about all that excellence stuff. It all comes down to the attitude we each have toward our work, how much we care. And as I've said, the attitudes that help in our work help in everything else, too.

I recently heard a physician discussing how people recover from serious illnesses. He said, "Those who do best are the ones who are able to work." Of course he mentioned other factors also, such as family support, but there was "work" right in the midst of it. He's saying that work is good for us, it's healthful.

Our work is such a privilege and such an important opportunity to express ourselves, gain satisfaction, and contribute to society. Amid the everyday hassles, let's never lose sight of the big picture.

HOW WE MAKE OTHERS FEEL

In our interactions with others, we need to be alert and sensitive to how we make others feel. It's very important.

How do we effectively give people feedback of any kind? This relates to the previous subject of *motivation*. When we want to give someone a message, how do we do it effectively?

What about criticism? Dale Carnegie says that criticism is futile. That is, it doesn't do any good. He says, "No man ever criticizes himself for anything, no matter how wrong he may be. Criticism is futile because it puts a man on the defensive, and usually makes him strive to justify himself. Criticism is dangerous, because it wounds a man's precious pride, hurts his sense of importance, and arouses his resentment."[5]

Benjamin Franklin was considered tactless in his youth but became one of the most outstanding diplomatic leaders of all times. He said, "I will speak ill of no man, and speak all the good I know of everybody."[6]

Before Charles Schwab started his investment firm, he was an executive with a steel company, where he was renowned for his ability to deal with people. He said, "There is nothing else that so kills the ambitions of a man as criticisms from his superiors. I never criticize anyone."[7]

We're not dealing with what's kind or unkind (but you can deal with that yourself). These experts are telling us that, based on their vast experience, criticism is just not effective in accomplishing things through others. You may feel that you have to criticize others as part of your work. Are you really sure? If an outstanding diplomat like Franklin and an outstanding executive like Schwab didn't have to criticize, and even found that it was a bad idea, do you really have to criticize on your job?

Columnist Ann Landers reported many people's experiments with avoiding expressing criticism and negative comments for a period of time, usually one month. People have tried it with a spouse, friend, or co-worker. Clearly, these people had already discovered that their criticism was not effective in accomplishing change, or anything else, with the person involved. So they thought they had nothing to lose by trying one month with no criticism. What they were surprised to learn was how effective the change was. What they had failed to accomplish in years of criticizing they accomplished rather quickly by not criticizing.

I worked on the stage crew for a play that was performed at our church. The director had been warning the actors that they had to learn their lines well or they could freeze up, forgetting what to say, and have a terrible experience on the stage. At the dress rehearsal a teenage boy did just that. He forgot his lines and suffered for what must have seemed an eternity to him. It was painful just watching him squirm. He eventually came up with something and the play moved on. After that act of the play was over, the cast and crew met, and the boy wasn't there at first. Everyone was wondering what the director was going to say to him. He slipped into the back of the room late and looked like he was trying to find a hole to hide in. I guess he expected to get a reaming and a big "I told you," but when the subject came up, the director just gave some tips, from her own experience, of what to do when that happens. She didn't "get on" the boy at all. When you think about it, what would be the point of getting on him? He already feels terrible about it and will be going over his lines feverishly to be sure it doesn't happen again. All the other actors are now frightened into doing likewise. So the point has been made and the experience has provided all the benefits it can.

If we do have to correct someone, we need to remember the adage "correct in private, commend in public."

The opposite of criticism is praise, so if criticism is ineffective then praise must be effective in dealing with others. Fulton Oursler[8] defines the following three principles of the art of praise:

1. *Realize the human need for praise.*

2. *Compliment sincerely.*

3. *Train ourselves to look for the praiseworthy.*

We're not talking about insincere flattery or manipulating people. This is sincere recognition of good qualities of another person, conveyed to him to give him a boost.

We tend to take people's good points for granted, and to focus on their weaknesses. We need to change that. We can always find things to praise or compliment in others, and it's important that we do so. Not just because it's beneficial to him, but because it strengthens our rapport with him.

We're wise to be alert for opportunities to offer sincere

compliments. Don't say anything you don't truly believe, but look for something positive on which to comment. In addition to directly complimenting the person, you can compliment something dear to him. If you're at someone's home, look for something you like and mention it. If the person has children, look for something you admire about them and mention it. Complimenting his or her spouse is great, too.

Praise is related to *appreciation*. We need to show people that we recognize their value and truly appreciate the good that they do. Why? First, because it makes our own life more rewarding and enjoyable. And second, because it really does help others.

A woman retired after teaching high school for over thirty years. At her retirement ceremony, someone asked her, "What is it that you remember most about all those years of teaching?" I'm sure the people present expected some answer related to the rewards of teaching.

She replied, "That none of the kids ever said 'Thank you.'"

Why is it that we're so negligent in offering thanks to people who help us along the way or who are just nice to us? Sure, we thank people for obvious favors and gifts. Maybe with teachers we think, "That's their job." But it's more than a job to them, at least to most of them. They do it to help young people. They do extra things, and their contributions are so important.

One simple way we can encourage others and have a positive influence on them is to express our thanks, i.e., our appreciation, for the good that they do. We can thank volunteers, good neighbors, friends, co-workers who give us a hand or some good advice, or anyone we have any dealings with.

One way to show that you really mean your thanks is to say it again sometime after the event. As we leave a party, we all thank the host, but that's so "expected" that it doesn't have much impact. By all means do it, but if you really want to show the host that you enjoyed the party, call him a few days later and thank him again. We all thank someone when he gives us a gift. But if you really want him to know how much you appreciate it, tell him sometime later how much you've been enjoying the gift.

When someone does some work for you, remember to thank him for that before pointing out what he didn't do or asking him for something else. I appreciate it when the person calling to ask for a contribution starts by thanking me for my past contributions.

Another way to show appreciation is to inform a person of the end result of his assistance. If he helps you prepare a talk, tell him how the talk went. If she helps on a project, tell her how well-received the final product was. People don't like to feel like their work disappeared down a black hole. They want feedback. If they see how their contribution really mattered, they will be more receptive to helping next time.

When we ask someone to do something for us, we can do it in a way that gives him or her a little verbal pat on the back. "You're really good at this sort of thing" or "I know with all your contacts you can find just what we need" shows we appreciate his or her abilities (as well as the help).

One step beyond appreciation is *encouragement*, which is one of the greatest human needs. Most of us need encouragement more than criticism. Criticism may destroy evil, but it does not propagate good. Criticism is like a surgeon's scalpel. It cuts away problem tissues, but after the operation a person needs wholesome food, restful sleep, and perhaps mellow sunshine to bring back the glow of good health. Appreciation and encouragement are the food, rest, and sunshine of the soul.

Many years ago, along the coast of Labrador, a severe storm came up very suddenly. The many fishermen out in small boats made a mad dash for the harbor. All of them made it except one man, older than the rest, who was known in the village as "Old John." As Old John was trying to get to the harbor a huge wave had thrown his small boat against a large rock, smashing it. By good fortune, Old John was not hurt and managed to climb onto the side of the rock. It was slippery, and very difficult to hold onto with the waves crashing into the rock. The villagers saw what had happened, and considered all means of rescuing Old John. But the storm was so intense there was no way they could get a boat out to him. They knew there was nothing that could be done. Old John would have to hang onto the rock until the storm subsided.

One of the villagers had an idea. He said, "We all know that Old John is going to have a terrific fight tonight until the storm subsides. Let's build a bonfire here on the shore that John can see. We'll throw our hats in the air every now and then just to let him know we're pulling for him." So they did. All night long the storm raged and the fishermen kept the fire going and kept tossing hats into the air.

The storm didn't subside until early the next morning. As soon as they could, the fishermen sent a boat out to the rock and rescued Old John. He had made it, but just barely. He became exhausted from hanging onto the rock while being pounded by the waves. He said that several times he almost gave up and figured it was his time to die, but then he'd look at the bonfire again, and the hats being thrown into the air. He thought, "If those guys care enough to spend the night out in this storm for me then maybe I won't give up yet." Tossing up a hat of encouragement in a storm seems a strange way of helping someone. But it saved a person's life.

SEEK OPPORTUNITIES TO PRAISE, SHOW APPRE-CIATION, AND ENCOURAGE OTHERS. — Key 7

Beyond encouragement, sometimes we need to give *hope.*

On December 7, 1996, the powerhouse Nebraska football team was a three-touchdown favorite over the University of Texas. Before the game, the Texas coach gave a very unusual talk to his team. He told them that millions of people would be watching the game on TV, and among those millions would be a lot of people who had more or less given up on life for some reason. Maybe some who were crippled or otherwise physically unable to lead a normal life. Maybe some who had lost their jobs and had little hope for meaningful work. Maybe some whose relationships with former loved ones were now nonexistent. Maybe there were some with a long history of failures, some who'd made a big mistake, and who knows what others. The coach said that maybe some of these hopeless people would turn on this game just to see what would happen to this three-touchdown underdog team. Maybe the underdog team could send a message of hope to all those people. Show them that it never pays to give up.

A message of hope through a football game? Sure! And how many other ways might we transmit a message of hope to someone who needs it? Maybe not to hundreds or thousands of them at a time. Maybe to just one at a time.

By the way, Texas won 37 to 27.

Jerry told about attending a piano recital in which his sister participated. It was held in a large auditorium, and there was a large audience. When her turn came, she played fine for about the first half of the piece, but then she forgot the next notes. She became very flustered. She backed up in the song a couple times, trying to get past the bad spot, but to no avail. As she was struggling, some of the other students started giggling. That caused a few more to join in, and a few people in the audience too. She improvised a bit, which sounded bad, somehow got to a better spot in the song, and finished. She hurried off

45

the stage, found a corner, and cried. It wasn't so much that she had messed up, but that people had laughed at her. It was the laughter of ridicule. That was the last piano recital in which she ever participated.

Would you think that in a book on interpersonal skills I'd need to say that we shouldn't ridicule people? Sometimes we think it's just good humor to make fun of someone. What, can't he take a joke? But there's nothing funny about hurting someone. It's unkind, and it's the worst thing you can do when building rapport and effective interpersonal relationships.

How do we make people feel? Do we make them feel good about themselves? Do we show that we appreciate them and what they do? Do we encourage their efforts and give them hope for the future?

HOW OTHERS MAKE US FEEL

There's a flip side to how we make others feel. It's also important for us to be alert and sensitive to how others make us feel, because how we feel affects our interactions with them.

Earl worked with me at one time. We really didn't work together, just at the same place. We didn't have much in common; there was a big difference in age and background although we did share an interest in boating. Earl was such a friendly, outgoing, happy guy. Always kidding. Always including everyone in the conversation. I just enjoyed being around him. He made me feel welcome, like he was really glad I was there, like he really liked me. I felt like he was an old friend.

Some people, like Earl, make us feel comfortable and put us at ease so that we interact freely with them, but other people make us uncomfortable for some reason. We feel nervous and ill at ease around them and sometimes feel like avoiding them. When we feel that way, we need to ask ourselves why we feel that way. What is it about this person, or the way we view him, that causes the uneasiness? Is it because we think he's likely to disagree with us or put us down? Does he easily fly off the handle? Do we think he's going to show us up and make us feel inferior? Do we think he'll embarrass us? What has happened in our past interactions that makes us fearful of future interactions?

Once we've figured out the reason for our uneasiness, we can counteract it. We can get things into perspective and mentally prepare ourselves for the coming interaction. We need to overcome the natural tendency we have to avoid contact just because of our uneasiness. Otherwise, we could be passing up opportunities that could benefit both the other person and ourselves.

Although we're wise to prepare for interactions we think may be difficult, we need to avoid overdoing it, however.

A man was driving down a country road late one night when a tire blew out. As he went to put on his spare, he discovered that he didn't have the jack that was normally stored in the trunk. He had taken it out for some reason and forgotten to put it back. He looked down the road and saw a farmhouse and thought, "Maybe that farmer can loan me a jack so I can change the tire." He started walking toward the house. He thought, "It's pretty late for me to disturb that farmer." About then, he saw the few lights on in the house go out. He thought, "I guess the farmer's gone to bed. Now I'll be getting him out of bed. He's not going to like that." He started walking faster, while thinking, "He'll have to go in his nightclothes and get the jack for me, and he'll probably feel like he has to stay up until I return it." As he approached the house he thought, "This guy's really going to be mad about this." As he rang the bell he thought, "He's going to tell me off for disturbing him at this hour. I shouldn't have come here. I should have gone on to a gas station, no matter how far it is." As a light came on inside, he thought, "He doesn't have any right to yell at me like just because I tried to borrow a jack." When the farmer opened the door, the man yelled at him, "You can take your old jack and shove it!"

Have you ever thought out how a conversation will go, preparing for the worst? *First I'll say this, then he'll come back with that objection, then I'll say ...* and so on. You've got the whole battle planned, and you're ready for the victory. Sometimes it turns out as expected, and you're glad you prepared. But other times, his first response is completely different from what you expected, and there's no confrontation. You feel relieved but maybe also a bit let down because you did all that worrying and preparation for nothing.

Robert took over as the leader of an organization I was involved in. He was a nice guy and very good at the job, but somehow he just made me uncomfortable. Conversation with him was always a bit unnerving. Maybe it was because he was so gung-ho about doing his job that he made me feel like I wasn't doing mine well enough. At one meeting, some things happened that made me feel badly about my role in the organization. I left the meeting feeling like he was running things as if he didn't need me. I was feeling sorry for myself, thinking maybe I'd quit and join another organization where I'd be appreciated more. I changed clothes and started to take a run. Maybe the exercise cleared my head, for afterward I felt like I needed to talk with him to straighten things out. I cut the run short, changed clothes again, and went back to the meeting room. Robert was still there, alone, putting things away from the meeting. I offered to help him get the room back together, and as we worked we talked. It wasn't unnerving this time. I realized that he did appreciate what I did for the organization, and I left feeling much better. I was so glad that I'd gone back to see him. Our relationship was much better after that.

If we want to have effective interactions with others, we need to make them feel at ease, and we also need to make ourselves feel at ease. When interacting with someone is difficult, we need to fight the natural tendency to avoid those interactions. We need to make that extra effort.

If we interact freely with people when things are going well, then we'll be able to interact effectively with them in more difficult times. If you have regular friendly chats with your neighbor, it will be a lot easier to deal with him when your kid hits a baseball through his window.

CONSIDERATION

I watched a teenage boy on his driveway preparing to wash a car. He got out the hose, bucket, and sponge, and began the first rinse of the car. As the first water runoff reached the gutter at the street, the boy noticed that it was turning left, heading for a street drain at the next corner down the street. The water would flow along the gutter past the neighbor's house, where the neighbor was cutting his grass. He knew that the grass clippings stick when there's water in the gutter and you can't clean them up until it's dry. It's a minor irritation. The boy realized this and ran to turn off the water. He moved the car over to the right side of the driveway and resumed the rinse operation, taking notice of the water's path. As he evidently expected, now when the water reached the street it turned right, heading for the drain at the corner in the other direction. Now it would flow only past the boy's own home and wouldn't bother the neighbor.

It seems just a little thing, but I thought about how wonderful it would be if we all would be so alert and sensitive to the ways in which our actions impact others, either positively or negatively. We should be willing to change our actions to improve those impacts. It's a matter of being considerate of others.

You've probably seen that sign that says:
If you get it out, put it away.
If you open it, close it.
If you turn it on, turn it off.
If you empty it, fill it.
If you get it dirty, clean it.
If you break it, fix it or get it fixed.

I've also picked up the following principles that go a step further:
Don't make a mess, even if I'm not the one who has to clean it up.
Don't waste money, even if it's not my money.
Don't cause other people unnecessary trouble.
Leave things better than I found them.

What do these things have in common? They help me to be considerate of others. In a broader sense, they help to ensure that I'm making a positive contribution to the world, not a negative one.

What kind of person doesn't care if he makes work for others, like leaving others to clean up after him? One who thinks he's so good that someone else should do his dirty work. That's what I think of when I see someone throw litter out of his car.

When you need to borrow something, ask for it, or if he's not there, leave a note. It's courteous, considerate, and ensures that you'll have future access to his resources.

Let's contrast the following two people:

Person A	Person B
Stands blocking other people's passage so they have to ask to get by.	Notices that others are having trouble getting by, and makes it easier for them.
Drives slowly on the freeway, oblivious to the long line of cars he's created behind.	Notices what's going on around him.
Pulls up to the closest gas pump, making others pull around him or back into the ones in front.	Doesn't inconvenience others.
Walks in front of the vehicle that dropped him off, so it has to wait for him to pass.	Walks behind the vehicle so people don't have to wait for him.
Plays loud music at the beach, assuming he has the right to select the music for all within earshot.	Respects other people's space.
Borrows things when you're gone without leaving a note. Has to be asked to return them.	Respects other people's property.
Is habitually late, keeping others waiting.	Respects other people's time.
Stands around when there's work to be done, waiting until he's asked to do something.	Sees what needs to be done and does it without being asked.
Walks off empty-handed, letting someone else carry the grocery bags or suitcases.	Does his or her share.

Some may say that Person A may not really be inconsiderate but just not observant and perhaps a tad lazy. But I maintain that noticing our impacts on others and doing our share in group activities are important aspects of developing effective interpersonal relationships. And you may say that how we treat strangers is not relevant to our interpersonal skills, because we're not trying to have effective relationships with them. But good or bad habits in dealing with strangers carry over into our interactions with people with whom we want to be effective.

We're wise to be considerate of someone's situation and feelings when we ask him to do something for us. We can say:

"I know you're busy, but ... (I hope you can do my job soon)."

"I know this isn't the most enjoyable kind of work for you, but ... (I hope you'll do it anyway)."

He will be more likely to do what we ask if he thinks we understand his situation and feelings. It shows that we care about him, not just about what we want.

We can be considerate in the things we say to others. But we can also be considerate by what we *don't* say. We can avoid saying something that will hurt someone, and that includes situations when the subject isn't present. Have you ever been in a group and they started talking about someone in a negative way? Did you try to steer the conversation away from negative gossip?

What if you had a real gem of gossip about the person, something you know they'd love to hear? It would make you the "star" of the gossip session. Would you have the good judgment and courage to keep it to yourself? It's been said that maturity involves the ability to have money and not spend it, and to have power and not use it. I think we should add, "to have information and not disclose it."

BE ACTIVELY CONSIDERATE OF OTHERS. — Key 8

We need to be active rather than passive, proactive rather than reactive, in considering other people's situations. We need to stay alert, seek out opportunities, and develop good habits.

USING RESOURCES

The most valuable resources in any enterprise are the human resources, and we have such a hard time managing those resources. We need to know the resources that are at our disposal, and we need to make the most of what we have.

I know one thing that particularly bothers older workers is that the "young bucks" running the show don't know what the veterans have done and hence what they can do. Not that anyone should live in the past, rest on his laurels, or expect that someone owes him something for all that he's done. We all need to continue to contribute as fully as possible to the current enterprise. But do supervisors really know the backgrounds and capabilities of their subordinates? Do they read the personnel files and talk to people to find out who has done—and can do—what? Do we tend to assume that each person is just good for doing what he's doing now? Do we pigeonhole people? Do we succumb to stereotypes? Do we allow, and expect, change and growth? How can we manage our human resources if we don't know what they are?

We've all read that human beings only use a small fraction of the capabilities of their brains. More generally, people only develop and use a small fraction of their capabilities. The challenge in every enterprise is to find ways to help people use more of their capabilities for the good of the enterprise. The ways in which we interact with people affect how fully they use

53

their capabilities, i.e., how productive they are. If our interactions with them cause them to be less productive than they could be, then we're wasting our resources, and these days that's something no organization can afford to do.

BE SURE YOU REALLY KNOW THE HUMAN RESOURCES YOU DEAL WITH, AND MAKE THE MOST OF THEM. — Key 9

COACHING AND MENTORING

One thing we generally don't do well in companies is when coaching employees. We hire the best people we can get, give them a little orientation, and then let them "sink or swim." Sure, we do performance appraisal and counseling, we assess their performance, strengths, weaknesses, and development needs, we sit down with them once a year and discuss this with them, and if they have problems, we may talk with them occasionally between those sessions. But do we really coach them to become more valuable employees?

Think about what the coach of an athletic team does. He works with his athletes every day, going over the fine points, in order to improve their performance. He ensures that they focus on the critical skills. practice extensively, think positively, and strive to be the very best they can be. He's demanding, but also supportive. Do we do that with our employees? We appreciate the importance of a good sports coach, and we see how teams fight to get the best coaches. Is coaching given that kind of importance in our company?

Gary Parker, the Director of the Stanford MBA program, says that the higher the education and skill level of the people working for you, the more you need to be a coach rather than a general.

The most important decision we need to make about an

employee is: "Is this employee a keeper?" If he's not, let him go now and stop worrying about him. But if he is a keeper then see to it that he gets the coaching to make him as valuable as he can be. Sure, it takes time to coach someone, but the benefits should outweigh that.

Some coaching should be done by the employee's immediate supervisor, but an effective adjunct to this is using a *mentor*. This is an experienced employee who works with the new employee to teach him the fine points and "tricks of the trade." A mentor can really help a new employee, but there are two important cautions: First, the new employee must not be treated as a "flunky" of the mentor. He must have responsibility for his own work and must not be made to feel like a second-class employee. He should value his relationship with his mentor, not resent it. Second, mentors must be chosen very carefully. Not all experienced employees are good at this or enjoy it. Since the objective is to pass on the work ethic, attitudes, and practices of the mentor to the new employee, it is essential to ensure that what is passed on is what we want to have passed on. A mentor should be selected only if he or she truly wants to do it.

A mentor and his protege need to form a special relationship based on mutual respect, trust, and caring. The mentor needs to take an interest in all aspects of the protege's life, not just work-related aspects. Both parties should be free to terminate the relationship if it is not working out, so that a better match can be found.

Obviously, coaching and mentoring is not just for corporations or athletic teams. It's needed in all sorts of everyday interactions. Do we really coach our kids (in matters other than sports)? Remember the general description of coaching above. Do we coach our spouse? Do we serve as a mentor to our kids? Are we really doing all we can to help those we love to get the most out of life?

SEIZE OPPORTUNITIES TO HELP OTHERS BY COACHING AND MENTORING. — Key 10

LEADERSHIP/MANAGEMENT STYLES

Those in leadership positions should be careful about what kind of communication atmosphere they create. And this includes not just "bosses" but anyone who has a position of authority over anyone else (and all of us do). If you get after people unexpectedly for things they say, they'll become very guarded in their conversation with you. If you yell at them when they bring you bad news, people will avoid bringing you bad news. They'll hide the bad news and problems from you, so you'll be making decisions on the basis of incomplete or inaccurate information. If you focus on people's mistakes, you'll force people to hide their mistakes from you or focus most of their energy on avoiding mistakes rather than doing positive things. If you jump all over those who disagree with you, you'll be surrounded by "yes-persons" who just tell you what they think you want to hear. You'll drift further and further out of touch with the real situation, and your subordinates will know you're out of touch. If you create an atmosphere of fear, you'll have a smooth-running machine that's going nowhere.

If you only talk to people when you have a gripe about something they've done (or haven't done), they'll dread contact with you. If you talk with them regularly and praise their work when things are going well, then they'll be more receptive to solving a problem when one arises. If the only interactions are negative ones, they won't be very effective. We need to build rapport before we can make corrections. If you treat people well when they communicate openly and honestly with you, then that's what they'll do.

It's helpful to think about the various management styles or approaches with respect to their impact on the attitudes of the workers. What is comes down to is, whatever the system emphasizes and rewards, that's what the employees will do. The results do not always lead to maximum productivity, which is the real goal of any enterprise.

What about "Management by Objectives?" Certainly it's good to have objectives, to set goals, and to assess progress toward them, but it's easy to get too caught up in the process. The problem is that this kind of system tends to emphasize results that are easily measurable, while neglecting less measurable aspects. Some things are micro-managed, while others are ignored. It's easy to get caught up in "bean counting" and tracking of targets, deliverables, and such things that get written down. When employees feel that their future depends on how well they meet these targets, they'll focus on meeting those targets to the letter but perhaps not always in intent. They can meet targets by neglecting other work, and increase quantity by taking shortcuts that decrease quality. They'll become very careful about setting targets. Only very attainable goals and limited-vision projects will be suggested. Creativity and long-range outlook will suffer. People can become cynical about what the organization values.

What about "Management by Exception?" Here the idea is that the manager can pay little attention to the majority of the work that progresses satisfactorily but should just focus on straightening out the things that are not going right. Seems like an efficient approach. The problem is that it leads to the manager constantly looking for "who's screwing up today." This, of course, makes the employees focus on not screwing up. Avoiding mistakes is laudable, and very important in some fields, but too much concern about that detracts from positive aspects of getting things done. An atmosphere can be created in which employees are very cautious, devoting a lot of time and energy to covering their rears and making excuses, Feeling that success depends not on how much good you do but how well you avoid screw-ups. Employees feel that all their good work is not appreciated, but one foul-up is disastrous. It's an atmosphere of fear.

Douglas McGregor's Theory X and Theory Y explains that there are two opposite assumptions about human nature and motivation, and they lead to different ways of managing others. Theory X assumes that most people prefer to be directed, are not interested in assuming responsibility, and are primarily interested in safety and security. They are motivated by money, other benefits, and the threat of punishment. Managers who have this view will closely control and direct others, and watch carefully for screw-offs, screw-ups, and other situations for which punishment is appropriate. In contrast, Theory Y assumes that people are not, by nature, lazy and unreliable. They can be basically self-directed and creative if properly motivated. Managers who have this view see their role as unleashing the potential in individuals, allowing them to achieve their own goals while directing their own efforts toward accomplishing the goals of the group.

Research has shown that the management pattern that follows from the Theory Y view is more effective at accomplishing the group's objectives. That's why management theory advocates this approach. Not because it's nice for the employees, or less stressful, or whatever, but because it's more effective. And it's no surprise, in view of what we learned about the Pygmalion effect.

Let me tell you a true story illustrating the Theory X view. Will was a laboratory technician who was very skilled at his work and had done it for over thirty years, but he was very hard to get along with. He was cranky, obnoxious, and had lots of idiosyncrasies. He wanted to work alone and plan and schedule his own work. His bosses adapted to his style by leaving him alone as much as possible, and he got the work done his way.

Then came a boss who couldn't handle the idea of a subordinate who wouldn't always do what he was told. There was a high priority, high visibility project, and the boss was worried that Will wouldn't get it done on time, so he instructed Will to work on nothing else until it was done. Will knew he could squeeze in some other work too, so he did. When the boss learned that Will wasn't working full-time on the big project, he got mad. He wanted to punish Will. He hired a contract technician, who had much less experience than Will, to finish the project, and reassigned Will to another area. He told everyone he didn't want Will near the lab where the big project was being done because he was afraid Will would sabotage the work.

The boss didn't know it, but Will went into his old lab several times early in the morning before going to his new assignment, but it wasn't to sabotage anything. He checked the equipment and made minor adjustments so that the best results would be obtained. This thirty-year veteran had been kicked out of his lab and replaced, but he still cared enough about the quality of the work to put in this extra effort. Amazing? No, what's amazing is how prevalent the Theory X view remains in spite of all the evidence refuting it.

Again let me emphasize that "management" refers to any process in which one individual has authority over someone else. It's good for all of us to think about what tendencies we might have to assign easily-measurable tasks rather than what's most important, or to focus on negative rather than positive performance, or to make negative assumptions about people. Think about the effect this has on the other person. Is this really the best way to get him to do his best, particularly in the long term? Is there a more human-related leadership/management style that will be more effective?

**CREATE THE KIND OF COMMUNICATION ATMOS-
PHERE THAT'S MOST EFFECTIVE FOR
ACCOMPLISHING YOUR OBJECTIVES—AN OPEN,
HONEST ONE. — Key 11**

LITTLE THINGS

I can't help but mention some "little things" that smooth our interpersonal relationships. Maybe they pale in importance compared with the major keys I've been discussing, but they do make a difference, and some effort on our part is all that's required.

The first is using people's names. We all know that people like to be called by name and that we should do so, but still we tend not to use names as much as we should. People say, "I can't remember names well." The truth is, we don't put much effort into it. When people are introduced, it's common for someone not to grasp the other person's name and not want to ask him to repeat it. You'll never remember it if you never knew it to start with. When you're going into a situation where you're going to be introduced to people, like a meeting or a party, focus on catching their names. Say the name to yourself several times while looking at the person's face. Write it down as soon as you can. Go over it throughout the meeting or party. Call the person by name a few times soon after meeting him. Look around the table or room, putting a name with each face.

Anticipate situations. When you see a familiar face approaching, try to come with his name before he gets to you and you speak to him, so you can call him by name. Sometimes a few seconds of thought is all it takes, but if you're not thinking you won't come up with it (at least until after he's gone). When you go to a meeting or party, think about who's likely to be there so you'll be ready with names. When you get a phone call, expect that the caller will identify himself first (which is proper phone etiquette) and be prepared to catch his name (and write it down) so you don't have to ask for it later.

Get both names so you don't have to sound formal by calling her Mrs. Smith just because you don't know her first name. When you list names, like in a program or meeting agenda, include both names so people will know what to call each other. If you need to use initials you can include the first name also, like D. W. (Doug) Hissong. If a person you're encountering has children that you've met, think ahead about the kids' names so you can ask about them by name (instead of "your son"). Parents love it when you ask about their kids.

Take initiative and be creative. If you have just some information on a person but want more, such as his or her spouse's name, children's names, etc., is there some organization's directory or phone book in which you can look them up? Write down names rather than trusting your memory. Keep a little book of names.

One Sunday in church I noticed a couple sitting a few pews ahead of me. He worked where I did, and they used to live close to us so we used to see them occasionally. But they moved overseas for six years, so I hadn't seen them for a long time. His name came to me easily, it was George. There he was, sitting with his wife, what's-her-name. I kept looking at the back of her head trying to think of her name. All sorts of names came to me, but I knew none of them was right. Shortly before the service ended, it came to me. Her name was Ruth. I was so pleased that I'd come up with it. As I left the room and turned a corner I came face-to-face with Ruth. I said, "Hi, Ruth, it's good to see you." And then, of course, I greeted George. Thank goodness I'd done my head-scratching to come up with her name before I needed, instead of afterwards.

If you know someone's name but don't think he knows yours, go ahead and use his name. It will make him more likely to learn yours.

If someone calls you by the wrong name, provide the correction in a very low-key manner, like it's no big deal. Don't just let it go or you'll perpetuate the error.

Another matter is using the correct form and pronunciation of the name. There's an easy way to find out how someone pronounces his name or if he prefers to be called Bob or Robert, James or Jim, etc. Just listen to how he says it when he introduces himself to someone or when he answers the phone. It's so simple. There's no excuse for irritating someone by getting his name wrong.

The second item is smiling, speaking to people, and being pleasant. We fuss over our hair and clothes, etc., to try to look good, while we ignore the simplest thing we can do to make ourselves look better, and that is to smile. Try this: Look at yourself in a mirror with a straight-faced expression (no smile). Study what you see, and think about how others react when they see that. Now change just one thing—add a nice smile. Not a phony or overdone smile, just a happy smile. Now think about how others react when they see that face. See the difference? See how much better you look? See how much more impact you'll have on people? The smile does a lot more to make you look good than all those other things you fuss over. Make a positive, pleasant attitude your default. Only be negative or grumpy when you really have a good reason to be. Your composure affects the way people treat you and respond to you. It's contagious, so use it to your advantage. You can make a difference!

Do you like it when people you know walk past you without speaking? Do you like being around people who always look like they're mad about something? Of course not. So why would you present such a front to others? You want people to gravitate toward you, not away from you. You want to attract, not repel. So be conscious of the way you look to others and how that affects your relationship with them.

The third thing is courtesy. Courtesy is just a means of showing respect for others. It's not old-fashioned and it's never out of place. It doesn't conflict with modern views of gender. It's part of your interpersonal relationships.

BE THE KIND OF PLEASANT, POSITIVE, SMILING, COURTEOUS PERSON THAT OTHERS ENJOY BEING AROUND. — Key 12

ROLES

The minister looked out over a packed congregation one Sunday and told them that the church obviously had outgrown its sanctuary and would need to start a fund-raising drive to build a new one. After the service a nine-year-old girl, Ida Lee Chapman, came up to see the minister. Out of her little Sunday purse she took a silver dollar and explained that she'd been saving it to buy something very special. She had decided the new sanctuary was something very special and she wanted to donate her dollar. And so the fund raising began. Two years later Ida Lee became ill and died. The sanctuary was completed in 1913. It has a number of beautiful stained glass windows. Under one of them is a plaque dedicating that window to Ida Lee Chapman. Ida Lee's role was that of a *starter*, getting things going

A man stopped on a street corner to admire a magnificent temple that had recently been built there. A young girl walked up to him and, noticing what he was looking at, asked, "Do you like it?"

He replied, "Oh, yes, it's beautiful."

The girl said, "I helped build it."

"You did, huh? How did a little girl like you help build that temple?"

She replied, "Well, my father was one of the bricklayers on the temple, and every day when he worked here I'd bring his lunch to him."

Yes, she did help build the temple. She found a way to do

her part. She played an important *support* role.

Earl Campbell was a star running back for the Houston Oilers years ago. He set records for yardage gained, and played a major role in the team's victories. On at least one occasion, he bought Rolex watches for the offensive linemen who worked with him. They opened up holes for him to run through and kept defensive players away from him. The fans cheered for Earl and knew he was great. Most of them probably never noticed what those linemen were doing. But Earl knew how important their role was, knew he couldn't have gained all those yards without their help, and he wanted to show his appreciation.

A friend told me about a role he had on the football team during his sophomore year in high school. During practice, he would wear the number of, and play the part of, the best running back on the team they were going to play the following weekend. That way the defense could practice tackling him. Evidently the defensive players took delight in tackling him hard. That was an important role in preparing the team for the coming game.

When I watch and hear a band or orchestra perform, I sometimes think about how each musician's role is so essential to the overall performance. Somehow it's particularly apparent for the percussionists, which is what one of my sons was in his high school band. At times they have significant periods in a song during which they don't play, but then a part comes up for them, and it must be executed just right. The timing is crucial for a percussionist.

My son's band was primarily a marching band, but they also performed two concerts per year in the school auditorium. For one of those concerts, we were running a bit late. He said he had to be on time because his band was playing first and because, "Well," he said, "You'll see." Sure enough, very near the beginning of the first song there was a bit of a pause, then a crash of the cymbals, done by our son. It was great. We knew what he meant. There may be a lot of kids in the band, but a song could be ruined if just one of them were to miss his or her cue.

Soccer has become a popular game in this country, and all my sons played it a number of seasons, starting at a young age. They each had some experience playing goalie. It's a unique position in that it doesn't involve the nearly constant running and kicking as do the other positions. When the ball is near the other end of the field, where you want it to be, the goalie has nothing to do. Sometimes the kid playing goalie sits down and plays in the dirt. The kids say it's boring at such times, but when there's a lot of activity in front of the goal, the goalie has to concentrate like no other player on the field. He has to be ready to spring into action any second to block a goal. It's a stressful position, because the goalie feels responsible if a goal is scored against him.

One of my sons was on the crew team at Cornell. His event involved eight men rowing one of those skinny boats. He picked up the sport quickly his freshman year, and by the spring of that year was the "stroke man" on his boat. In addition to the eight rowers, there's a coxswain who's a small individual (there's a weight limit on him) who sits in the stern, steers the boat, and directs the rowers by setting the pace, etc. He faces forward so he can see what's going on, whereas the rowers face the rear. The stroke man is the rower sitting next to the coxswain. His role is key in setting the pace, because he's the rower who can be seen by all the others. The stroke man must know what he's doing, and has a leadership position somewhat like that of the quarterback on a football team. It's a high-visibility position. When the team wins, the reporters interview the stroke man. He can revel in the glory.

During his sophomore year, my son moved up to the

varsity boat, and by spring of that year he was stroke man on the varsity boat. He quickly pointed out that there were stronger rowers sitting behind him. Indeed, a few seats behind him was a senior who was nationally recognized at that time and later rowed on the U.S. Olympic team. That senior had been the stroke man in previous years. Now he was sitting in the part of the boat they call the "engine room," where the major power is developed. During his junior and senior years, my son also rowed in the "engine room." It takes years of work to develop the kind of power required for that.

Some roles involve more show and glory than others. At times we may enjoy the spotlight and the leadership roles, but we need to appreciate that sometimes we can make even greater contributions by less-flashy, behind-the-scenes work that provides the real power for major accomplishments.

Texas A&M University, which one of my sons attended, has many traditions, among which is the "Twelfth Man." It originated back in days when football teams were much smaller. In a championship game in 1922, A&M was struggling with a narrow lead. In the first half they'd had so many injuries that the coach wasn't sure he'd have enough players to finish the game. He called into the stands for a student who had left the football team earlier in the year to play basketball. The student willingly donned the uniform of one of the injured players and joined the team on the bench. He didn't have to play but was the only one left on the bench when the game ended (A&M won). His readiness to support his team even to the point of entering the scrimmage inspired the tradition. The A&M student body, known as the Twelfth Man, stands by their team, ready to serve when needed. For the second-half kickoff, a Twelfth Man representative, i.e., a non-scholarship athlete from the student body, is placed on the kick return team. He's one of the primary receivers, and when he gets to return the kickoff everyone goes wild. Some roles involve *standing by* in case we're needed.

A former pastor of our church, Don, once served a church that was trying to buy an organ. They had tried various means to raise the money but were still far short of the amount needed. Don knew of a man in the community who was wealthy enough to solve the problem, but didn't know how he could convince him to make the large contribution needed. He clearly had no interest in doing anything significant for the church. Don asked Allan, a member of the congregation who was a close friend, to talk to him. Allan carefully planned how he would bring up the subject and ask about the contribution, and the man agreed.

Allan's role was that of a *facilitator*, and he was in a unique position to do this task because of his close relationship to the wealthy man.

When the time came for the seventh graders to try out for those few, highly coveted positions as school baton twirlers, Beth was more than ready. She'd been taking twirling lessons for a year and a half and had been practicing a great deal. She performed at the tryouts and anxiously awaited the judges' decision. When the winners' names were read, Beth's was not among them. She and her mother cried a great deal. It took a long time for that hurt to subside.

The next year when the seventh graders showed up for the twirling tryouts, Beth was there to share her story. She cried with the ones who didn't make it. She realized that because of her experience she could give those kids something that few others could give them.

Sometimes we're in a rare position to make things happen, and sometimes if we don't do it, it won't get done.

I worked with a woman named Margarita who likes to snow ski at Taos, New Mexico, a small town with a big ski area known for its challenging slopes. Margarita was skiing there once with a friend when she fell and broke her leg. Margarita went with her friend to a doctor in town, who set the leg with such efficiency that Margarita commented on it to the doctor. He replied, "Lady, do you have any idea how many of these I do every year?"

When my wife was pregnant with our third son, a friend referred her to a young doctor. He liked to use the latest technology, like ultrasound. But my wife decided she wanted a conservative doctor, so she chose a doctor who was at least sixty years old. She said, "You know he's been doing this all his life." I'm sure he'd delivered a lot of babies by that time. There's something reassuring about all that experience.

There are a lot of people who do excel in their careers, even though they're not famous or even well-known. In many cases they excel because they just keep after it year after year and keep looking for ways to make small improvements.

Many people make frequent changes in their career work in the early years, then settle into doing similar work, something they're really good at, for a long time. Their role is that of a *master*.

The NASA Space Center headquarters is close to Houston. Many NASA employees live in the town of Friendswood, which is just south of Houston. Don, the former minister of our church, had previously been at a church in Friendswood. One of the members of that congregation was the head of the NASA Space Center at that time. As such, this man was very well known in government circles. He was on a first-name basis with the President and several cabinet members and frequently lunched with top officials. But when their church needed some work done on a sewer line he volunteered. Don said he vividly remembers watching the distinguished head of the Space Center up to his knees in mud, working on the sewer line. Sometimes we play different roles that vary widely.

In our interactions with others, we all have roles to play,

and it is very important that we recognize them and play them well. Sometimes our role is to get something started, sometimes it's a support role, providing key behind-the-scenes performance that makes the team succeed or perhaps just standing by for a brief, but crucial, job. Sometimes we're in a unique position to help someone or enabling someone else to do something. Sometimes we're the master.

As we get older, we tend to derive more satisfaction from what we accomplish through other people. Sometimes we can help others do things we cannot or will not do ourselves. We may be instrumental in helping someone be hired, or getting someone to join an organization, who will go on to do great things for the company or organization. We may help train someone who goes on to major accomplishments. Our children are obvious examples of ones we help to make contributions. In all these cases, it's satisfying to us, and, after all, what we help others do is really a part of our own contribution to the world.

INCREASING OUR IMPACT ON OTHERS

There are three kinds of people: those who don't know what's happening, those who watch things happen, and those who make things happen. Someone has to make an effort in order to make something happen. We all want to have more influence on events around us and have a more positive impact on others. We need to be alert to opportunities and willing to put in some effort.

Finding Opportunities

Nowhere do we have so much potential for impact as in volunteer organizations. The quality of life in our communities is directly affected by many organizations that depend on volunteers either entirely or to supplement the efforts of some paid staff. What some people accomplish through their volunteer efforts is amazing!

In the wee hours of one morning I suddenly awoke with an excruciating pain in my side. I knew it was serious. I staggered around the house a bit, writhing in pain, then I vomited a couple times. I knew I needed to get to the emergency room, but could never drive myself there so I dialed 9-1-1 and managed to mumble enough words to tell them of my problem. Within ten minutes there was a man at the door who said the ambulance was on the way and he was a paramedic who would help me in the meantime. He started taking my "vitals," and within another five minutes a woman arrived to help him. Within another five minutes the ambulance had arrived and a crew of uniformed men loaded me onto a stretcher and rushed me to the emergency room.

At the hospital I was examined and X-rayed. Then, rather suddenly, the pain went away. It was a kidney stone. After a couple of hours at the hospital I went home. No more trouble.

I never received a bill for the paramedics services or the ambulance ride. In our area, the ambulance service, as well as the fire department, are volunteer organizations. We contribute through our water bills for the equipment they use, but the people are unpaid volunteers. Those people left their homes and families in the middle of the night to help me, as they do others, and they didn't get paid a cent for it.

On a Sunday afternoon we were having a severe thunderstorm. We were startled by a very loud clap of thunder and a simultaneous flash of lightning. Since the lightning and thunder occurred together, I knew it hit close, and I commented to that effect. About ten minutes later, my son came running in to tell us that a house down the street was on fire. We ran outside and saw flames leaping high into the air. Neighbors were gathering fast. A fire chief car was there, so I knew the fire department had been notified. The volunteer firemen started appearing in their own cars. One parked in our driveway, quickly opened his trunk and put on the gear he had stored there, and ran to the fire. Then the fire trucks came, with more men on board. All volunteers, there in the rain risking their lives to fight that fire.

I've known some of our volunteer firemen/paramedics over the years I've lived in this area. My hat goes off to all of them. They're people who really care about helping others and making our community a better place to live.

I've noticed that in any organization run by volunteers you can get as much responsibility as you want if you're just a little patient and willing to invest time—you can be president of any of these organizations. How's that for an ego boost? It's true. All you have to do is start attending meetings regularly and show that you're willing, even anxious, to help out. They'll keep giving you more responsibility until you rise to the top. In some organizations it will happen more quickly than in others, but you'll get there. Anyone who is bored or complaining that he has nothing to do or is not appreciated is just not looking in the right places.

People who have studied career "burnout" have found that burnout is not caused by overwork or stress, but by boredom. Boredom is a self-imposed condition.

A kindergarten teacher had a song she loved doing with her classes. It was called the "Popcorn Song." The kids squatted down, then at the appropriate time began popping up and down like popcorn popping. But one time a boy just stayed squatted down. She asked him, "Why aren't you popping up?" He said, "I'm just burning on the bottom of the pot." Are we popping up to do things or just burning on the bottom of the pot?

Again, I'm convinced that we all have, and can have, more influence in the world and more positive impact on others than we might realize. None of us is a small cog in a huge wheel. We can accomplish a great deal if we want to. There are opportunities all over the place available for our choosing.

I like the following item:

"Do you xvxr fxxl that you'rx not important—that you'rx just anothxr kxy in lifx's typxwritxr? Wxll, just sxx what happxns whxn only onx kxy is missing. Substitutxs can bx madx but thx rxsult is nxvxr thx samx." —C. W. Caldwell

When you have young children you hear a lot of children's songs, which often have really significant messages if you just get past the cuteness and think about the words. A prime example is the song "*Sunbeam*," which includes the refrain:

A sunbeam, a sunbeam
Jesus wants me for a sunbeam
A sunbeam, a sunbeam
I'll be a sunbeam for Him.

Do the little kids appreciate what they're singing? Picture a cold, dark room. Then through a window comes a bright, warm sunbeam. It makes the whole room so much more pleasant; the people in the room feel better. The song says that we're supposed to act like sunbeams, bringing cheery, warm brightness and comfort where it is lacking. What a wonderful idea! We need to be alert for opportunities to do that, and to take advantages of those opportunities.

Small Positive Steps

There was a death in a family and, as usual, many individuals called or stopped by to express their sympathy. Many of them told the widow, "If there's anything I can do to help, please let me know." A boy who knew the family showed up at the door carrying a box. He expressed his sympathy, then said, "I'm here to shine your family's shoes." The widow was puzzled, so he explained, "Well, you'll be receiving a lot of guests and attending a funeral and you'll all want to look nice and you don't want to be bothered shining shoes right now. So I'll do it for you."

After the funeral and related activities were all over, the widow reflected on all the offers of help. She appreciated the thoughtfulness of everyone. She never asked anything of those who had made general offers to help. But she really appreciated the fact that the boy had identified a specific need and had taken care of it.

A woman was shopping in a downtown area when she saw a young boy standing on a sidewalk grate trying to keep warm. It was a cold day, but he was barefoot and had no coat. She took the boy into a store and bought him shoes, socks, and a coat. He was so excited he started to run home to show his mother. But halfway down the block he stopped, turned around, and came back to the woman. He asked, "Are you God's wife?"

She thought a moment, then replied, "No, but I'm one of His children."

Then the boy said, "I knew you were some kin of His."

John Capoletti was a star football player for Penn State University. 1973 was a particularly outstanding year for him, and he not only made the All-American team but also won the coveted Heisman trophy. The Heisman trophy is essentially an award for the best college football player in the United States. It's awarded at a very fancy ceremony in New York City. When John received the Heisman trophy, he immediately gave it to his younger brother, Joey. Joey had leukemia and couldn't participate in sports like his big brother. He lived in constant pain. John admired his little brother so much for his courage, attitude, and what he was doing with his life that he thought Joey deserved the Heisman. John's act of selfless love clearly had a profound influence not only on Joey but also on all who witnessed it. The story is told in a movie titled *Something for*

Joey.

Most of us have too many "I could"s. When we see a need we think, "I could do this," and, "I could do that." "Could"s are always plentiful. We need a cure for the common "could." Convert those "could"s into "will"s. Pick out the best ideas and pledge that you will put them into action. Convert possibility into reality.

They say the road to hell is paved with good intentions. Some people have enough good intentions for an eight-lane superhighway. We need to convert our intentions into actions.

We ponder about whether we should do this or do that. We need to come in out of the *whether*. We need to take action.

Making a Difference

A man was walking along a beach. Far ahead he noticed a person repeatedly moving back and forth between the water's edge and the area farther from the water. As he got closer he noticed that it was a young woman who appeared to be picking things up from the drier beach, then going to the water's edge and throwing them out into the water. When he got to where the girl was, he paused for a moment to watch, but still couldn't see what she was throwing into the water, so he asked her.

She replied, "These starfish have washed up onto the beach and are stranded by the falling tide. This hot sun may kill them, so I'm throwing them back into the water to save them."

The man watched a bit more, then said, "There's miles of beach here, and probably thousands of starfish washed up on it. You can't possibly make a difference."

The girl picked up another starfish and threw it out into the water. She turned to the man and said, "It made a difference for that one."

The man walked on. But he kept thinking about what she had said. Before long he returned and, alongside the girl, began throwing starfish out into the water.

W. Edwards Deming was the "guru" of modern management principles dealing with enhancing quality in the workplace, primarily by restoring the dignity, self-esteem, and proper role of the individual. Shortly before his death at the age of 93, Deming was leading a four-day seminar in Houston. His health was so poor that he had an oxygen tank strapped on to aid his breathing, but he was still wheezing and suffering as he led the seminar. During a break one of the participants came up to Deming and said, "Dr. Deming, why don't you just knock off this afternoon and get some rest? Everyone here will understand." When Deming declined, the man became somewhat flustered and asked him, "Why do you torment yourself like this?"

Deming replied, "To make a difference."

We all have talents we can use to make a difference for others. We need to develop and use those talents, focusing on what lies ahead rather than what has passed. The question is, "Are our talents tools or trophies?" Something we use, or just something we reflect on?

Diana, Princess of Wales, worked in numerous ways to help the homeless, ill, and otherwise less fortunate persons of the world although her position didn't require it. She could have spent all her time with the rich and famous instead of spending some of it with the down and out. The song Elton John wrote for and sang at her funeral spoke to this side of her. It mentioned how she "whispered to those in pain," and referred to "the wings of your compassion" (Diana's). But perhaps the greatest tribute to Diana's style came from a woman in a homeless shelter, who was interviewed after Diana's death. "She came in and talked to us like we were ordinary people and she was an ordinary person."

By and large, real accomplishment comes from repeated, sincere, one-on-one interaction with others. Something we all have ample opportunity to do.

Being There

I know I've missed a lot of opportunities I should have taken advantage of, and I want to do better. I remember one case where I, with my wife, did the right thing:

When I started to work full-time, I joined the company at a "boom time" when a lot of people were starting. I'm glad there were a lot of us, because there's a camaraderie among people who start work together that is most enjoyable. There were lots of parties and activities. A few of us even lived in the same apartment complex for the first year. It was nice.

In this group was Robert, a friendly, outgoing, guy who took an interest in everyone. He always asked lots of questions. As you might expect, he and his wife, Bonnie, developed a lot of friends. They were invited to every party or event. My wife and I were among their many friends.

After a few years, the "boom time" turned into a "squeeze time," and some reduction in force started quietly occurring. Robert had had some problems on the job, and he was let go. I was somewhat of a leader of his at the time, so I was told a short time before it happened. He was so embarrassed that he told no one. Friday, his last day of work, passed without a word. The next evening, curiosity got the better of my wife and I, and we drove by their house. Every light in the house was on. We assumed they were packing and didn't have the courage to stop in.

Monday morning the office was buzzing with comments like, "What happened to Robert? He's gone." Everyone soon found out. Somehow we learned that Robert and Bonnie had gone out of town for a couple of weeks to do some job interviewing and to "recuperate" a bit with relatives.

When those weeks plus a couple more had passed, we drove over to their house. This time we had the courage to stop in. Although they were obviously glad to see us, this visit wasn't as pleasant as the many others we'd had. There were a lot of tears from Bonnie, and some from the rest of us. Bonnie commented that they hadn't seen anyone else since it happened. I thought, "Where are all those friends of theirs now?" Fair weather friends, I guess. (By the way, Robert went on to other successful jobs.)

Pass It On

I enjoy boating, primarily because for us it's usually associated with water skiing. It just happens. On one occasion when we were out on the lake, skiing, I returned to pick up a fallen skier in the usual manner, and cut the engine as he boarded the boat. I re-started the engine, but when I pushed the lever for "forward" the boat didn't move an inch. I thought maybe seaweed was wrapped around the propeller, although with that I still would have expected a little action, so I stopped the engine and got in the water behind the boat to check the prop. I was amazed to find that there was no prop. It was gone! I didn't know that could happen. Evidently it was not installed properly and came off when it hit something. With no propeller we couldn't go anywhere. We tried a bit of searching for it on the bottom until it became clear that it was hopeless.

We flagged down a passing boat and asked if they might give us a tow to the nearest launch ramp where we'd find a way to get to our car and trailer at the end of the lake. They insisted on towing us all the way to where we had launched. It must have taken over half an hour. I offered to pay the driver for his gas and for his time and trouble. He wouldn't take any money but said, "When you see someone who needs help, you can help them." I've thought a lot about that since. You repay a favor by doing one for someone else. You "pass it on." What a wonderful idea! I promised myself that I would.

On another trip to that lake some time later we were flagged down by a family in a boat that had run out of gas. They asked for a tow, and of course I agreed. They told us that others they had asked said no. It was a fairly long tow to the nearest dock with a gas pump, but I didn't mind. They offered to "top off" my gas tank but I said, "When you see someone who needs help, you can help them."

Our local paper recently carried an interesting story about a couple who stopped for lunch at a restaurant in our area. They enjoyed the meal, but had quite a surprise when the waitress brought their check. It said, "No Charge." Accompanying the check was a note from a man who had stopped in and anonymously picked up their check. The waitress said he did that from time to time. His philosophy is that if he does something nice for someone, perhaps that someone will do something nice for someone else. The couple said they intended to pass on that lovely good deed.

The idea of performing "random acts of kindness" is growing. At tollbooths, people sometimes pay the tolls for several cars behind them. What a wonderful trend!

Using What We Have

Woody Hayes was the football coach at Ohio State University for a very long time, and a very successful one. He was a colorful figure. I think it's a shame that many people remember Woody mostly for his sideline displays of temper. They don't know the other side of Woody. He had a very positive influence on the lives of a large number of young men whom he inspired. Because he was a "celebrity" in Columbus, he knew that people liked to see him. He used that fact to do a lot of good in the community. He spent a lot of time visiting people in hospitals. I once ran into him in a hospital in Columbus. He influenced a lot of lives.

Sharon lives in my area. People kept telling her that she looked like the Disney character Snow White. A few years ago she dressed as Snow White for an office Halloween party. Her co-workers got a kick out of it, but what really surprised her was the reaction of a group of children who saw her in costume after the party. The experience gave her an idea. She thought about cheering up sick children. When a local children's hospital held a fund-raising telethon for a large number of such hospitals, Sharon appeared as Snow White. She saw joy light up the faces of somber children. She felt like their long-lost friend. I'm sure a lot more ailing children will be enjoying visits with Snow White.

Mother's Day was approaching, and a pre-school teacher asked her students why they loved their mothers. Most of the responses were of the sort the teacher expected, including various things that mothers do for and with their children. But one response caught the teacher by surprise. One girl replied, "I love my mother because she removes the thorns from the roses so I can hold them." Do we ever remove thorns for someone else's benefit, particularly to bring beauty to them?

Dorothy was widely renowned for her work with troubled people. She had, for many years, devoted her life to helping people. Her reputation was so great that a magazine reporter named Eric arranged to meet with her to learn more about her great work. When he arrived at her place of work and asked, he was told that she was in the kitchen. He went to the kitchen and found her talking with a man who was obviously very drunk. The man was also unbelievably filthy—Eric could smell him and the liquor all the way across the room. Eric didn't want to interrupt, so he waited quietly inside the door. Dorothy talked with the man for about ten more minutes, then, when she rose to leave, noticed Eric standing by the door. She asked him, "Do you want to speak with one of us?"

"One of us?," he thought. "Would I want to talk to that filthy, smelly, drunk?" But Dorothy placed that drunk at the same level as herself. Maybe that attitude is what made her so effective with others.

A priest and a rabbi got together for a round of golf. It didn't take the rabbi long to figure out that the priest had spent a lot of time on the links. He played very well. His putting was particularly impressive. The rabbi noticed that the priest made the sign of the cross before each putt. On the second nine, the rabbi asked the priest if it would be okay if he too crossed himself before putting. The priest said, "Sure, rabbi, go ahead. But it won't do you any good until you learn how to putt."

We tend to look for someone or something that will give us what we're looking for, but usually we just need to buckle down and do it ourselves.

There's a song with a great title: *"Take your candle, go light your world."*

Transmitting

I think television is amazing. Not what's shown on it but how it works. Invisible waves are sent out from transmitters. The TV stations have no idea who's going to do something with those waves. They don't know if we're watching a particular channel or not (unless we're in the Nielsen group, and who knows anyone who is?). We have no clue that the waves are all around us until we turn on a TV set, when we can tune in whatever channel appeals to us at the time. The picture and sound magically appear.

We're all "transmitters" of sorts, constantly sending out

messages by what we say and do, and we have no idea who's going to pick them up, or if anyone has picked them up or not.

We're all "receivers" too. We "flip the channels" picking up bits from here and there. The senders have no idea what we've obtained from them, but everything we absorb becomes a part of us.

Fleeting Moments with Permanent Impacts

I saw a ballet titled "Fingerprints," which was supposed to explore the dynamic interactions that take place whenever people meet. The choreographer said it was "to express the profoundly personal way we all leave our mark on others and upon our surroundings. Just as fingerprints are unique to each of us, we touch others' lives in a unique and individual way with our personalities and talents. Everyone is changed—even minutely—by simple interactions. Even the most subtle of gestures—a passing smile from a stranger, a bad mood expressed while waiting in line, a cheerful exchange between friends or an intimate embrace—all leave a definable finger-print." I can't say that I could discern all that from the dancing, but I certainly believe the message.

As we think about our day-to-day impacts on other people, we need to keep in mind how permanent those impacts are. The human body is an unbelievable creation, and one of the most amazing parts of it is the brain. People often compare the brain with a computer because of its ability to process and store information. It's been called the "necktop computer." There's a similarity, but the brain is much better. For one thing, it doesn't conk out during electrical power surges and inter-ruptions. And there's an important difference when it comes to storing information. A computer has a definite amount of storage capacity. It may be large, but every item you put in takes up some of that space, and when it's full you can't add any more. You hear school kids talk of their brains in that way, like

"I don't want to fill my brain up with this useless stuff because I need room for the practical stuff."

But from what I read, the brain is unlike a computer in that there is no limit to how much information it can store. The more we put in, the more it increases its capacity. We don't have to worry about filling it up. Since new information doesn't displace old information, there's no limit to how long something can be stored in our brains. We all remember some things from long, long ago, while at least appearing to forget other things quickly.

I'm not much into gardening, but there's one thing I've learned about it. If you want your plants to thrive, you must keep the weeds out. It's not just that weeds look bad. The real problem is that they take up nutrients and water such that the plants suffer. Certain things in life are just better excluded.

I belong to the Masons, a wonderful organization. The Masons have a rule that there are no alcoholic beverages at Masonic functions. It's not that Masons are teetotalers, but rather realize that alcohol causes problems for some people and hence it's not consistent with the Masons' objective of "making good men better." A lodge I formerly belonged to had a custom of following one special meeting every year with a meal of oyster stew. Every year the recipe was passed along to the person in charge of the cooking. One year a group of us were standing around chatting after eating the stew. The cook said that he had considered using a different recipe, one that included some whiskey. He thought that since the cooking would boil off most, if not all, of the alcohol maybe it would be O.K. for a Masonic function. But he wasn't sure, so he used the old recipe. Some of us were thinking that he probably should have tried the new recipe, when a visitor spoke up. He said, "I'm sure glad you didn't do that, because I'm a recovering alcoholic and that would have set me way back." We didn't know what to say. I guess we'd never thought about the possibility of such an innocent thing causing such a problem for someone.

Our personalities are based on all the experiences we've had during our lives up to the current time. Thinking of that, plus the potentially permanent memory we have, we need to be a bit cautious of what sorts of experiences we subject ourselves to. And we need to be careful about what kinds of experiences we're subjecting other people to.

PEOPLE I'VE KNOWN

There are some other aspects of interpersonal relationships that I thought I could best convey by introducing you to some people I've encountered along the way. People who've given me something special.

George was the father of a girl I knew in high school. He was an undertaker who had a good sense of humor, which included joking about his occupation. When a group of our gang needed transportation to a party or on a triple date, George would take them in a hearse. It was roomy, and it took your mind off the stigma of being driven by a parent when you were too young to drive yourself. One older woman in our church used to joke with George about how when she died he'd fix her up so beautifully for the funeral. They'd joke about how he'd get the perfect color and style for her hair. George spent his working life making people look their best for their funerals. He was good at it.

Then George died. But no undertaker had a chance to make George look good for a funeral for he was killed in a plane crash. It occurred high in the air, and the pieces of his body were spread so widely they couldn't even be found. Sad, and ironic. What we do for others is very important.

Sherwood was the father of Chip, who was on the high

school swimming team with me. Chip and I were co-captains one year. Sherwood was a "wild and crazy guy." At the swim meets, when the swimmers stepped up onto the blocks, the audience would get quiet for the start. When Chip was in the race, his dad would let out a big "ape call."

When we graduated from high school, the ceremony was held at Cincinnati's ornate Music Hall. In the midst of the solemn ceremony we heard—you guessed it—a giant ape call. Then, after the ceremony, as the new graduates rejoined their families in the entrance hall, hundreds of people watched in amazement as Sherwood repeatedly bowed at his son's feet, pleading with him to get a job and get out of the house. A little wildness and craziness spices up our lives in a delightful way.

A former co-worker of mine, Doug, got married on a boat—not a cruise ship, just a relatively small dive boat. He and his new wife loved water sports, and both were on the wild-and-crazy side. The captain married them. Doug wore a tuxedo, and his bride a full wedding gown. Immediately after they were pronounced husband and wife, they grabbed snorkels and dove into the water. They ruined the wedding clothes, but created a lifetime memory much more valuable.

I don't know if I thought about it at the time, but in retrospect I see that my high school had a class, or caste system. The "upper" class included good-looking kids from richer families (I presumed). Most of them belonged to the only one fraternity and one sorority for the upper class. They were in a lot of activities and dated each other in long-term relationships. I guess each of them was such a "prize" that they didn't want to give up such a great boyfriend or girlfriend.

I was in the "middle" class. It was the largest group, kids from middle class families (I think). These kids were heavily into activities, too. Those who were in fraternities and sororities were chosen from the middle class and dated within their class.

The lower class consisted of "hoods" who rode motorcycles and customized cars, plus the homely girls who hung around with them. It also included poor (I presumed) kids who rode the bus great distances to school (to get to those "poor" areas). They weren't in any activities. Those who were in a fraternity or sorority joined one dedicated to this class. They also dated within their class.

Carol was in the upper class. We knew each other by name but never associated in any way because of the class difference. When I was in my third year of college, Carol transferred into my school. I ran into her on the campus and it was like running into an old friend. We had some interesting and enjoyable conversation and a lunch date. Nothing more developed, but it was enough to make us think a bit about the way we sometimes put ridiculous bounds on our relationships. Artificial limits that we may think make us special but that really just limit us. We build fences around ourselves to keep others out, but they also keep us in. When we avoid relationships we may think we're giving the message, "I have plenty of friends, so I don't need you," but the real message is, "I have a limited capacity for friendship and I'm already at my limit."

I had a lot of blind dates while I was in college. Really, my social life might have been the pits if it hadn't been for all the folks who fixed me up with various girls.

Cindy was one of my blind dates. Back then the yearbook of the University of Cincinnati had a section titled "Cincinnatian Beauties" that featured pictures of girls selected as the most beautiful on the campus. (They may not do it anymore; it seems like a sexist thing.) One year Cindy was in that section. Can you imagine having a blind date with someone considered a beauty queen? She certainly was beautiful, and I was awed at first. But as the evening progressed I began to see her as a beautiful china doll, on display for all to admire. She was so perfectly made up that I was afraid to touch her for fear of messing up or breaking something. I decided that beauty really was only skin deep and there were other girls who seemed more real and whose company I preferred.

Kathy was another one of my blind dates. We dated for several months. A number of times at the end of a date we'd be at her house talking or playing some game and we'd suddenly discover that it was about 3 A.M.. Some of the latest nights I ever spent were with Kathy. We seemed to be comfortable with each other. But something bothered me terribly about our relationship. It was platonic, like a brother-sister relationship, no romance. I didn't understand it, was embarrassed by it, and didn't know what to do about it. The real pity was that I never discussed it with Kathy. I just stopped dating her.

About a year later things took a new turn and I started dating her again. She said something about not knowing why we had stopped dating the first time. I passed up that opportunity to talk about it. After a few months our relationship had the same problem, I still didn't understand it, still didn't discuss it with her, and stopped dating her again. I'm embarrassed to admit that I made the same mistake twice.

It was years later before I came to see the lesson I should have learned from Kathy. Weaknesses in our relationships, which lessen the quality of our life and others' lives, result more often from what we *don't* say than from what we do say. I still find myself at times coming up short in this area. God help us to seize the opportunities we have and to find the right words to discuss the difficult topics with others.

Web was my research advisor in graduate school. He was renowned as an excellent experimentalist. His laboratory produced some of the best data of its type. He worked closely with his students to ensure that the quality standard was maintained. When it came to purifying the materials we worked with, Web would work all day with a student, carefully going through a laborious procedure to ensure very high purity. On one occasion, near the end of the procedure something happened that contaminated the sample. Web said, "Aw, shucks!" and began preparing to repeat the procedure the next day. In his book, there was no shortcut to excellence.

John, a manager at the place where I first worked after finishing school, used to say that engineers should negotiate a new contract with their employers every year based on their accomplishments in the last year—like baseball players. He always wore white shirts and bow ties, at a time when the rest of us wore pastel shirts and long ties. One year, on his birthday, all of us who worked for him came to work in white shirts and bow ties. He got such a kick out of it that he assembled all of us in his office and had a picture taken of the room full of guys wearing white shirts and bow ties. He invited his boss to be in the picture, also. His boss didn't know about the plan for the special dress, so he was wearing a blue shirt and a long tie. John enjoyed showing people the picture and asking them who the oddball in the picture was.

Sometimes when a project was really hot, John would sit in on our group meetings, which was most unusual. He said that was "participative management." I know of one case where he went out on a limb for me, and I certainly appreciated that. I had a great respect for him. Years later when faced with a management problem I'd sometimes ask myself, "What would John do?"

Years later I had the pleasure of working with another manager, Chuck. He was years ahead of the current fads on "empowering" employees, open communication, and non-threatening work environments. He was a good friend to his employees as well as a very effective manager and leader. He brought out the best in us. He showed us what we could do—

always more than we had thought. (There's that Pygmalion effect again.)

Ron went along on what I think was the first time I tried water skiing. I swallowed so much of the river while struggling to get up on the skis that it's a wonder I didn't get sick. Ron had only one arm, and one of his legs was noticeably shorter than the other, but he was an excellent water skier. His one arm was strong enough to hold the tow rope, and the fact that he used a single slalom ski made the difference in lengths of his legs less of a problem, I suppose.

More recently I was reminded of Ron by a young lady named Jill. She went on a water-skiing outing with a youth group from our church. Whenever a group I'm in any way connected to goes skiing, I invite myself. They're always glad to have another boat. Jill had only one leg. On the way to the lake, one of the kids in my car asked, "How can she ski with one leg?" We found out that she skied just fine. I guess Ron and Jill more than made up for some physical problems with an extra dose of determination.

Betty used to work where I do, and since we lived in the same subdivision we carpooled to work for several years. Every year at Thanksgiving she'd pick out a fairly new employee at work who had moved a long way for this job and hence had no relatives nearby for the holiday. She'd invite him to spend Thanksgiving with her family. What a thoughtful gesture!

When one of our sons was ten he was sledding down a hill and hit a tree. He remained sort of pale and lethargic, so we took him to a hospital emergency room. A nurse took him away as we completed the paperwork. When we saw him again he was on one of those portable beds and had an IV going in his arm. We were told that he had a ruptured spleen and that a surgeon had been called. Talk about terrified parents!

Soon the surgeon, Richard, showed up and examined our son. He could have made some money on removing the spleen, but Richard knew that ten-year old boys heal well and he wanted to give the spleen a chance to heal. We waited through a few anxious days, some of it in the intensive care unit of the hospital. The spleen healed, and no operation was needed. Sometimes what we *don't* do is very important. Thanks, Richard.

Ed, a former co-worker, told me that he had a conversation with an older man in our work group and was amazed at fascinating aspects to the man's life, things he would never have guessed from the man's quiet and serious mode at work. Ed said, "Man, there's layers to that guy." We're each like a big onion. Layer after layer.

People are fascinating and full of surprises. They're not always what they seem. There are reasons why they act or appear the way they do. There are ways to bring out "hidden" aspects. They're precious, and sometimes a bit fragile. We need to be careful with them. How wonderful it is to discover an unexpected aspect deep inside and bring it out for all to enjoy.

INTERACTIONS WITH SPOUSES

Since so many of us get married, I want to say something about the very important matter of interacting with our spouses:

Imagine that you're buying a house. At the closing, among that big stack of papers you have to sign, there's one that says that you agree to live in this house for the rest of your life. "What?" you protest. "That's crazy! There's no way I can agree to that."

The person in charge of the closing says, "What's wrong? Don't you like the house?"

"Of course, I love it, but I can't agree to live there forever. It may turn out that there's something wrong with it. I may get tired of it. My tastes or needs may change, and someday I might want something different, something better. It's great now, but the rest of my life? No way!"

When you get married, the vow you take is just like that. You agree to stay married to, and be faithful to, this person for the rest of your life, regardless of how you or this person or your circumstances may change.

When I got married, I didn't smile during the wedding ceremony. I know it bothered some people in the audience. I wish I could have smiled, but I couldn't. I smiled plenty at the rehearsal the night before, and during all the preparations right up until I walked into that sanctuary for the real thing. As soon as the ceremony was over I started smiling again. I smiled plenty at the reception afterwards, but not during the ceremony itself.

Looking back, I think I was struck by what a serious step I was taking, what an unbelievable commitment I was making. It was scary. I was right—deciding to get married and whom to marry is the most important decision you make. That's why those years of dating before marriage are such an important part of your life. Those dating experiences not only help you decide whether to get married and whom to marry, but they help you to understand persons of that other gender. They are different. After you're married your relationships with persons of the other gender are limited, so be sure you have plenty of experiences and close relationships before you get married. Make the most of those opportunities.

I'd advise anyone contemplating marriage to take plenty of time to get to know this person extremely well. Ask lots of questions and find out everything you can. Test this person and test your relationship. Be very sure! And be sure you've had plenty of experience with others to understand how persons of that gender think, and to provide comparisons with this person. This all sounds very crass and unromantic, but it's your life!

I don't think there's a "one and only" for each of us. There are a number of people with whom any of us could be happily married. We just have to find one of them; but the choice is so extremely important we need to give it all we have.

One reason so many people are willing to take the risks associated with marriage is that it can provide some very big rewards. The very commitment that makes it so scary is what makes it so wonderful.

In our subdivision newsletter, there's a section in which the editor interviews a resident. She uses a standard list of questions, one of which is, "What accomplishments are you most proud of?" I don't recall seeing an answer yet that didn't include, usually as the first item mentioned, something about a wonderful marriage of __ years to __. People always cite that as a major accomplishment. I guess they realize that a good, long marriage is something not everyone has and something that takes some doing. It takes some effort, sacrifice, and compromise. Those who feel they have a good marriage are proud of it, as they should be.

Marriage is the biggest commitment that we will make. Once we've made that commitment, certainly it's worth the effort to nurture the relationship with our spouse. No other relationship could be as important to us although any relationship requires maintenance (that doesn't sound very romantic). A crucial part of that maintenance involves a sincere effort to communicate effectively with our spouse.

Baylor University conducted a study of styles of communications between spouses. They examined couples who communicated well and couples who did not. We're all different, and generalizations are dangerous, but these researchers boiled it all down into one key area of emphasis for each gender: For wives, the key is to keep suggestions positive, avoiding any tendency to diminish or "nag" the husband. For husbands, the key is to truly listen to what the wife is saying, understand what she is feeling, and take her feelings into account.

When we are working on a conflict with our spouse, it's important to address the problem and not attack the person. We should discuss the specific behavior and why it causes problems, avoiding generalizing with "You always..." or "You never...." It's much more effective to explain how the behavior makes us feel. (By the way, addressing the problem rather than attacking the person is a good thing to remember in other situations, such as when we have to correct a co-worker.)

You may have heard the sayings, "Don't let the sun set on your anger" or "Don't go to bed angry." Anger tends to fester and worsen with time. Anger is bad for your health, i.e., it increases your blood pressure. Repeated anger can actually shorten your life. When you have a disagreement with your spouse, it's a great idea to resolve it before the end of the day.

INTERACTIONS WITH YOUNG PEOPLE

Since so many of us have children or otherwise deal with young people, I want to say something about the special nature of interacting with young people. The pastor of the church that my family belonged to when I was a teenager always referred to us as "young people." I suppose he thought that "kids" or "children" were too demeaning or something. We young people got a kick out of it.

My three sons have been, and continue to be, a tremendous joy to me. They're the greatest! Whatever good is going on with them may well be in spite of me rather than because of me, but I'll try to take whatever credit I can. From some of the things I hear from other parents, maybe my kids (young people) have been unusually good to me. I certainly don't have all the answers when it comes to young people, but I can share some things I've run into.

Adults should have more fun. We tend to take life too seriously. A major reason for generation-gap-type alienation between parents and young people relates to the fact that many young people don't see their parents, and other adults, having much fun. They see their parents working five days a week on their jobs and the other two days working around the house. That's all they do. No outside interests or regular fun. They take maybe a two-week family vacation once a year, but that's it. When I look at some people I think I'm seeing the modern version of what Thoreau meant when he wrote, "The mass of men lead lives of quiet desperation." The young people look at their parents and say, "Is this what I have to look forward to when I grow up? No thanks." They try to find an alternative.

We all need to make room in our busy lives for some genuine fun, and it's particularly important that we have fun with our kids.

Did you see any of those ads the Mormon Church ran on TV, evidently to get us thinking about how we interact with our kids? I remember two of them:

A mother and daughter arrived home from grocery shopping. They were unloading the groceries from the back of the station wagon and carrying them into the house. The girl was old enough to be of some help with that. But she let one bag tip such that the pie on the top of the bag fell onto the driveway with a big *splat*—upside down, of course. When the mother saw that scrambled mess of blueberry pie, she probably thought of money wasted and no dessert for that dinner she had planned. The look on her face showed she was about to launch a tirade into the girl, but just in time, other thoughts evidently crossed her mind: *It was an accident; the girl certainly didn't do it on purpose. The girl obviously felt very bad about it already and would try to be more careful in the future, so what good would it do to get angry?* The next scene showed the mother and daughter sitting on the tailgate of the wagon, laughing, eating that jumbled-up pie right out of the box.

By the way, this matter of avoiding unnecessary confrontation applies to our interactions with adults also. We need to stop and think about what will be gained (or lost) by yelling at someone.

The second ad showed a father, clad in pajamas, heading for the door of a bedroom where his young daughter was obviously hosting a slumber party. There was a lot of commotion in the room, and he was clearly angry. He threw open the door and yelled, "Is there a pillow fight going on in here?" The group of girls, who were obviously doing just that, instantly fell silent. Then other thoughts quickly flashed in the father's mind: *After all, a pillow fight is pretty harmless fun. Why embarrass his daughter in front of her friends?* His frown turned into a big smile as he said, "Because I just love a good pillow fight!" The next scene showed him in there swinging pillows like mad with his daughter and her friends, amid the loudest laughter of the evening.

Both these parents turned what could have been an angry, and pointless, confrontation into a wonderful memory for their kids, and for themselves. And the kids saw that their parents like to have fun, too.

I read a brief item in "Reader's Digest" about a family at the end of a vacation at the beach. On the morning they were leaving, they hauled things from the house they'd rented and were loading up the car, having planned an early start because it was a full day's drive home. Then the parents realized that the two kids had disappeared. They yelled for them but got no reply. They went around the back of the house and saw the kids down at the beach splashing in the water, in their travel clothes, getting soaked. Their first thoughts were about how the kids would have to change out of those wet clothes before they left, how they were going to get a late start, and so forth.

They were angry as they started running toward the kids, ready to "let them have it" for their irresponsible behavior. But as they approached the water, some other thoughts came crashing in: *Clearly, it was hard for the kids to leave such a fun place. Most of the year was taken up with school and work and whatever else, and the family really didn't get many chances to really have fun together. A trip like this was a very precious time.* At the water's edge, the parents looked at each other and realized they felt the same way. They plunged into the water, clothes and all, and played with the kids in a way they had never done before.

Sometimes in our endeavors to teach our kids all the right things and set a good example for them, we neglect to teach them some of the most important things of all.

I've noticed that when you pack a suitcase, a box of Christmas presents, or load suitcases into the trunk of the car, it's best to put the biggest items in first. If you do that, you can always squeeze the little ones in around them. But if you pack the little things first you can never get the big ones in. It's the same with our time. We need to make room for the big items first, the things that take a significant block of time. We need to block out time for family vacations, weekend trips, and other major outings before the little day-to-day activities fill up our calendars such that we can't fit in the big things. I've also noticed that if we don't plan our own time, someone will plan it for us. That is, our calendar will get filled with little things that someone else thinks are important. Who's going to set our priorities?

We spend so much of our lives on routine activities, we need to remember to make time for the special moments with our loved ones, particularly our children and spouses. Those special moments are truly gems. Life is like a string of pearls. If you stop adding the pearls, all you have is a piece of string.

I've gone on a lot of campouts with my sons and other boys and their fathers, particularly though Indian Guide and scouting organizations. Some fathers enjoy that sort of thing; others avoid it like the plague. I particularly remember one father who wanted to go camping with a scout group. He was diabetic, so we altered our menu a bit. One cold morning I remember seeing him go out to his pickup truck to give himself an insulin shot. Now there's a father for whom camping presented some problems. He had a good excuse to stay home, but he wanted to be with his son and his friends sharing some experiences.

I went on a campout with a group of other fathers and sons when boys were about six years old. It rained for most of the weekend. The sun only came out for one afternoon, and we did some boating then. But I noticed something interesting about six-year-old boys. They don't know that it's not fun to camp in the rain. Maybe it's because they don't care if everything gets wet. They don't think about the mess of breaking camp in the rain and cleaning up everything afterwards; and since they don't know that it's not fun, it is fun for them. Fun is a matter of viewpoint, or attitude. In spite of the rain, definitely all the boys, and I think also the dads, were glad they went.

I read an article written by a man who recalled how he had complained about how much it was costing him to raise his son. Every year, as the boy grew older, his food, clothes, and activities cost more and more, and his father was really feeling the strain. Then the boy suddenly died. The bills stopped. The father said he would give anything to have the bills back again, he'd pay them with joy, if only he could have his son back, too.

A mother described how she cried when she had to buy her son his first wheelchair when he was at an age when she should have been buying him his first bike.

My father died a couple of months before our second son

was born, knowing our second child was coming. My mother died a couple of months after our third son was born. She knew of him and had seen pictures but didn't get to see him in person. None of us knows what it's like after death, of course, but I have a theory about Heaven: I believe people there know what's happening with their loved ones on Earth. It seems like that would be a necessary part of making it a pleasant place. I'm sure they're as proud of their grandsons as I am.

Our relationships with the young people dear to us are priceless. I remember three things my mother said about raising children: She thought the best age was around ten, when they are old enough to take care of themselves but not old enough to get into trouble. My brother and I must have been good at that age. She also said there was a good reason why God provided for people to have children while they are relatively young—so they can keep up with them. She said children are not given to us but rather are loaned.

I've enjoyed my sons immensely at every age. Every age has its own challenges and its own rewards, and it's interesting to watch young people change so drastically over the years. What they need from their parents changes so much—from diaper changes to bedtime stories, from homework help to rides everywhere, from using the car to lots of money for college. Their activities change—from the early years when any little thing you do thrills them, to the years when nothing short of a full day at an amusement or water park will satisfy them. They're so independent in some ways but so dependent in others. They're all different, but all wonderful.

In working with various youth groups, it's been interesting to me how much young people take after their parents, and I don't mean in physical appearance. When you find a kid who takes his or her responsibility to the organization seriously and strives to do his part, you'll find parents with similar attitudes. When the kid "bounces off the walls," usually at least one parent is sort of that way too. Children mirror their parents. As they say, "The apple falls close to the tree."

Young people go through stages in their attitudes about their parents. When they're very young they think Dad and Mom can do no wrong, but they grow out of that quickly. During the teen years they're amazed at how stupid their parents are, and a few years later, they're amazed at how much their parents have learned in those few years. I like the bumper stickers that say, "Hire a teenager while they still know everything."

As young people get older, they naturally become more independent of the adults in their lives. We can always support their efforts, encourage them, and offer them opportunities, but as they get older we lose our ability to make them do things. More and more, they have to make their own decisions, and benefit from or suffer from the consequences of those decisions.

We build our relationships with our young people one day at a time. Everything we do with them is one more little bond. I think back over all the activities I did with my sons as they were growing up. Those activities had short-term benefits in that they were enjoyable at the time, but I think they also had a long-term benefit in the kind of relationship we developed. And, of course, the process is continuing.

The home atmosphere we create is so important. A house is just a bunch of wood, sheet rock, and glass. We make it into a home when we fill it with love. Our homes should be refuges from the rest of the world, a place where we can say what we think and know that we are loved even when we screw up. We shouldn't expect perfect harmony at home, because people will always disagree, but the key is doing things and solving problems in a spirit of love and mutual respect. At home we get our "batteries charged up" to head out into the world to do things.

We can learn from our young people if we'll listen to them. A teenager I know has a father who's opinionated and has a short fuse. I witnessed a scene in which the boy started telling off his Dad about everything Dad was doing wrong in his life. I don't think young people should be disrespectful to their parents, but I do think they should feel free to express their opinions. In this case, what the boy was saying was true and I think his father needed to hear it. I was thinking, "Oh, the poor boy. His Dad is going to kill him." But his dad just listened. I was impressed. I'm sure it helped both of them and their relationship a great deal.

Parents should feel free to express their opinions, too, of course, and young people should listen to them. Communication is a two-way street.

It's difficult to communicate with teenagers at times. The typical parent/teen conversation tends to be like this:

"Where did you go?"

"Out."

"What did you do?"

"Nothing."

"How was school today?"

"Fine."

Teens are striving to establish their independence from their parents, and that sometimes means they don't want to have much to do with them or say much to them. But with some effort, we can get them to open up using some more specific questions, and some dialog that offers help rather than asking questions. Relating our own experiences and feelings can help. They really take more interest in what we say than they let on.

Teenagers often don't appear to have much interest in family activities, particularly family vacations, and act like they'd rather be somewhere else doing something else with someone else, and complain that they're bored. But later on you may hear them telling someone about it and you realize that they actually enjoyed it.

A high school girl was talking to a friend the week after the prom. She told her how she'd just "died of embarrassment" when her date brought her home about two A.M. and her mother was waiting up for her. She was totally humiliated. Amidst her ranting and raving about her "stupid mother," however, she noticed that her friend was crying. She asked her what was the matter. Her friend related that when she came home from the prom, no one was up, and the next day no one seemed to care either. She was crying as she thought how wonderful it would be to have parents who cared that much about her. Our kids may act like they wish we weren't around, but deep down they appreciate our love and concern for them.

Young people can help us to lighten up, open up, and shut up. The younger ones are great examples of innocence, curiosity, non-materialism, and appreciation of little things.

As parents, we're concerned when we see our children making decisions that will affect the rest of their lives. They make more of those as they get older. We can't make those decisions for them, but can only strive to give them the background they need to make them wisely. We can give them roots, values, and wings. Our goal is to produce individuals who will be able to live productive and happy lives.

A boy was fishing with his dad when he caught the biggest fish of his life. He was thrilled. It was a bass. Bass season would open at noon that very day. But now it was only ten A.M.. There was no one within sight of their boat, so no one saw him catch the bass. When they returned from the trip that afternoon no one would know whether the bass was caught before or after noon. They talked about it for a bit, then turned the fish loose. There was no compromising what was right. The boy said he never forgot the lesson of that day. This was a true story retold in "Reader's Digest" some time ago.

A father took his son to an exposition. The sign at the ticket booth stated the adult admission charge and the children's admission, but no age for the children's admission. The father asked the age limit for children. The young man working the booth said, "Twelve and under."

The father said, "We'll then it's two adults, since he's thirteen."

The young man said, "Did you just hit the lottery or something? You could have told me he was twelve and I wouldn't have known the difference."

The father replied, "But he would have and I would have." Our children learn from our examples, and we're like salesmen, never knowing which part of the demonstration will do the selling.

Young people need to see that their parents:

1. *Believe in certain things and are willing to stand up for them.*
2. *Take charge and responsibility to get things done.*
3. *Enjoy life.*
4. *Love their kids.*

At times I've wanted to write a poem about raising young people. The title would be "Someday." Unfortunately, I don't think I'm too gifted at poetry, so I haven't gotten far past the title.

I'll try to tell you about it in prose. (Or maybe this is one of those poems that doesn't rhyme, which I've never understood.)

Someday

Someday there won't be fingerprints on every window and mirror in the house. There won't be toys scattered on the floors and stairs. There won't be clothes, especially gym shoes, all over the house. There won't be closets I'm afraid to look into or beds I'm afraid to look under. There won't be little shoes that need cleaning, toys that need fixing, spills that need mopping, or scrapes that need bandaging. There won't be bills from pediatricians and orthodontists. There won't be birthday parties to give and to attend, campouts to go on, and events at the school. There won't be rock music in the air and pizza cartons in the game room.

Someday the house and the cars will stay neat and clean. The house will be quiet and peaceful. The cars will last longer. There will be time to read and to think. To think about what has passed. To give thanks. To miss it all. Someday.

We need to remember that a child is the only thing God can use to make an adult, and we are instruments He uses in making that transformation.

PART 2
COMMUNICATION SKILLS

ONE-ON-ONE COMMUNICATION

My secretary was helping me work on a report. It contained one figure that was rather "arty" with complicated boxes and arrows. I showed it to my secretary and told her I wasn't happy with the figure. I explained what I was trying to convey with it. She said, "Let me think about it and see if I can come up with something better."

The next morning when I came in I found on my desk a copy of her new version of the figure, and it was much better. It was just what I wanted, very clear and easy to follow. I went into her office beaming and said, "Hey, I really like your figure."

As soon as the words were out of my mouth I thought, "What a stupid thing to say." She gave me a puzzled look, but I guess neither of us could think of anything to say that wouldn't just make it worse.

That's the thing about oral communications, they're so fleeting. The speaker must come up with the words so quickly, and the listener has to capture them just as quickly.

Most of our communication is one-on-one with an individual, primarily by talking but possibly including notes we write to them. How we handle those one-on-one communications is very important to our effectiveness with others.

Although it's very important, there's not much to say about one-on-one communications beyond what we've already discussed regarding interpersonal skills. Interpersonal and communication skills, on the individual level, are closely linked. Our everyday conversations with individuals are a direct reflection of, and consequence of, our interpersonal attitudes and skills. Talking with others is how we interact with them, how we develop relationships with them, and how we influence them. If we keep focused on the other person and what's going on in his or her head, we'll say the right things.

Have you ever watched two people talk? It's a good way to improve your own conversational skills. When you're not part of the conversation you can be objective and focus on the interaction. Sometimes people talk *at* each other without really interacting. Sometimes they talk *past* each other. They take turns saying things but don't ask questions, and what they say is not affected by what the other person says, because they're focusing more on talking than on listening. Sometimes one person dominates the conversation such that the other person can't get a word in edgewise.

When we talk with someone, we need to be conscious of the process as well as the content. We need to ensure that the other party is feeling good about his role in the conversation. If we want someone to listen to us, we need to listen to him. He will get our message much better if he feels that it's a two-way communication and that we really care about his point of view.

Telephone Communication

We do a lot of communicating by telephone and recognize that talking on the phone is less personal than talking face-to-face. We hear what the other person says but can't pick up any clues from his face. Gesturing is mostly wasted, although what you're doing as you talk can have some effect on how you sound. Some advise that if you want to sound dynamic on the phone you should pace around as you talk. There's obviously no opportunity for touching. If the person has an accent much different from yours (you say you don't have an accent?) or your language is not his primary language, it's more difficult to understand the person when you can't watch him talk.

When there's a choice, we should think about whether it's better to call someone or to talk in person. I was working overseas on a short-term assignment along with one of the others from my company who was on one of many multi-week trips he made there. The day before he was to go home from this trip, his wife called him, halfway around the world, to tell him that she was filing for divorce. It was a complete surprise to him, and he was crushed. She probably thought it would be easier, but an important topic should warrant a face-to-face discussion.

Phone message systems make the telephone even more impersonal. When you leave a message, it's one-sided communication. It can be efficient if the other person answers your question with a reply message without even having to call back, but trading messages certainly is impersonal, and we need to be careful with it. Messages may be O.K. for transferring information, but when feelings are involved or some interaction is needed, we need to talk with the person.

Here are a few rules to make our phone communications more effective:

1. Identify yourself at once when you call. Don't expect anyone but your spouse to recognize your voice, and don't play guessing games.

2. Return phone calls promptly. Not doing so sends a negative message.

3. Think about whether to leave a message or call back. Don't leave a message if it's a subject that warrants a live conversation. Leave a message if it will enable him to prepare for the conversation, or get the information you're requesting and maybe eliminate another call.

4. If you leave a message, include your phone number. Make it easy for the person to reply. Although I don't agree, a co-worker once told me he usually doesn't return messages if there's no phone number.

5. Avoid protracted "phone tag." Don't leave messages requiring callback just before you're going to be away from your phone for a long time. If you misconnect a couple of times, don't keep leaving messages.

Electronic Communication

More and more communication is being done electronically, that is, by e-mail. There are obviously a number of advantages to this type of communication. It's certainly wonderful to be able to instantly send a message anywhere in the world. It's very helpful when there's a large time difference between the two ends, so someone doesn't have to call during the evening to catch the other person during the working day. It can help when there's a language barrier; the recipient can study the message instead of having to catch it rapidly while listening. You can keep a number of people informed by sending copies of the message. If the recipient of the message isn't the appropriate one to handle the matter, he can easily forward it to someone else. A record of the communication is kept.

But there are also some potential pitfalls to electronic communication, and we need to be careful about these. There is some tendency to overuse e-mail, perhaps because it's easy or it's fun. Sometimes it's not the most efficient way to communicate. People often spend more time typing out a message than it would take to make a phone call. People send e-mails to others just down the hall when they could more easily talk to them in person.

E-mail is less personal than a face-to-face conversation

or a phone call. It has a depersonalizing effect in the work environment. It's one-way at a time—one person puts forth his or her thoughts with no immediate feedback or give-and-take. The other person may respond, but then it's his turn at a segment of one-way communication. Since writing out the message is more laborious than talking, we tend to leave out the small talk, and maybe some of the courtesy, and just focus on the business at hand. If there's some criticism or expression of disappointment with how things are going, we tend to leave out the perspective with positive aspects and just get right into the negatives. One of my co-workers says that if you just trade e-mail messages with someone for long enough you'll make him mad. Sometimes we fire off an e-mail on impulse, and it shows.

The easy forwarding feature of e-mail is dangerous. If a message contains something negative about someone else, the message can easily be forwarded to that person. Or it can be forwarded to someone whose perspective is so different that he will get a completely different message from it.

Communicating by e-mail is challenging and risky. It's a form of written communication in which you have to get it right the first time. E-mails are usually sent immediately, with no "soaking" or "cooling off" period, no input from others, and no approval by your boss. Of course, you can pass the note to others for comments or approval before sending it, but for most notes we don't do that. It's easy to write something that irritates someone, or worse.

These suggestions should help make e-mail communications more effective:

1. Think about whether e-mail is the most efficient and effective way to communicate. Just because someone sent you an e-mail doesn't mean that's the best way for you to respond. Maybe a long string of e-mail messages needs to be interrupted by a phone call or visit.

2. Try to keep your e-mail messages as "friendly" as your personal and phone conversations. Remember to say "please" and "thank you." (Did your mother call those the "magic words"?)

3. Don't respond to an e-mail without thinking through the ramifications of your reply. If it has made you mad, give yourself a cooling off period. Print the message, read it again, discuss it with someone, then think about the beat way to reply.

4. Think about inputs and approvals you need before sending an e-mail. You can route a copy to someone for comments or to your boss for approval.

5. Think about to whom you should send copies, to keep everyone informed and to avoid offending anyone.

Before you hit the "send" button, look over your message, think how the recipient will react to it, and remember that you are in effect broadcasting this message to the whole world (at least everyone having access to your e-mail system). If you wouldn't want the president of your company to read it, don't send it.

Think about what the recipient will want to do with your message. Will he want to forward it to someone for action? Make that easy for him. That may mean separate notes for separate topics.

6. **Be considerate of the recipient.** Don't overload messages with attachments that are some trouble to handle and that can fill up someone's mailbox. Don't keep adding to and forwarding a note to extremes. Sometimes it's better to write a new note.

**CHOOSE CAREFULLY THE COMMUNICATION
MODE YOU USE: FACE-TO-FACE, BY TELEPHONE,
BY E-MAIL, OR IN WRITING. — Key 1**

Effects of Gender

A man was walking along a California beach and came across an old lamp. He picked it up and rubbed it and out popped a genie. The genie said, "O.K., O.K., you released me from the lamp, blah, blah, blah, yada, yada, yada. This is the fourth time this month and I'm getting a little sick of these wishes, so you can forget about three. You only get one wish.

The man thought about it for a while and said, "I've always wanted to go to Hawaii but I'm afraid of flying and I get very seasick. I wish you'd build me a bridge to Hawaii so I can drive over there to visit.

The genie laughed and said, "That's impossible! Think of the logistics of that. How would the supports ever reach the bottom of the Pacific Ocean? Think of how much concrete, how much steel. No way! Think of another wish.

The man thought a bit more and then said, "I've never been good with women. They always say that I don't care and don't understand and that I'm insensitive, so I wish I could understand women thoroughly... know how they feel inside and what they're thinking when they give me the silent treatment, know why they're crying, know what they really want when they say 'nothing', know how to make them truly happy."

The genie paused a moment, then said, "You want that bridge two lanes or four?"

A man asked his wife what she wanted for her birthday, which was the next day. She replied, "I'd like to be ten again."

The next morning he got her up early and took her to the amusement park. He made sure she rode every roller coaster and spin-'em, flip-'em ride in the park. Five hours later she staggered out of the park with her head spinning and her stomach churning. He took her to a fast food place for a burger, fries, and a shake. Then he took her to see the latest science-fiction horror movie, accompanied by popcorn and a drink. When they finally got home she collapsed in bed, exhausted and with a questionable stomach. Her husband kissed her and asked, "So how does it feel to be age ten again?"

She replied, "I was talking about dress size."

It's fashionable to talk about how men and women communicate differently. We need to recognize that it's dangerous to generalize, for we're all different, and some men and some women differ from the most common patterns. It's wise to recognize those patterns and be careful that they're not hampering communication with someone of the opposite gender (who could be your spouse). Here are the key general tendencies:

1. Men tend to emphasize problem solving, information, and advice, whereas women tend to emphasize feelings more. A woman discussing a problem may be simply looking for a sympathetic ear, but a man tends to think she's seeking a solution.

2. Women tend to ask more questions and to focus more on keeping the conversation going. Techniques for the latter include "uh huh"s etc. to indicate that you're listening and to encourage the person to continue, and conversational bridges such as "Yes, but...."

3. Women tend to use more language that promotes unity and "oneness" between those involved in the conversation. Women tend to emphasize agreement and consensus. Men tend to stand more alone in what they say.

4. Women tend to favor "talking a problem out" because that builds intimacy, whereas men are anxious to find a quick solution to eliminate the need for talking about it.

I must say that women tend to be better conversationalists. We men would be wise to pick up a few tips from them. But both men and women need to be aware of these different tendencies and to watch for their effects.

People tend to adapt their conversational style somewhat to the situation. Some people use a somewhat different style on the job because they feel it's more effective. For example, some women who work primarily with men converse more like men regarding the above tendencies.

The most obvious application of cross-gender communication is between spouses. Certainly, there's no one more important for you to communicate well with than your spouse.

LISTENING

A man spent years trying to teach his cat to talk. He'd never heard of a talking cat, and he figured he'd really have something great if his cat could talk. He tried every technique he could imagine, without success. One day he's sitting in the living room with his cat and the cat suddenly turns to him and says, "Look out!"

The man didn't respond, because either he didn't hear the cat or it didn't register that the cat had spoken. The ceiling crashed down, burying the man in a pile of rubble. The cat shook his head in disgust and said, "He spends six years trying to get me to talk and when I do he doesn't even listen to me."

A man who'd lived all his life in the country was visiting a friend who now lived in a very large city. The friend was showing him around the downtown area of the city at noontime. The streets were packed with people scurrying every which way, and there was lots of noise. The country man had never seen anything like this before. Suddenly he stopped and asked his friend, "Do you hear that cricket chirping?

The friend replied, "You can't hear a little cricket with all this racket."

Then the country man took a few coins out of his pocket and dropped them on the busy sidewalk. A number of people must have heard the jingle of those coins, because they scrambled to find and pick them up. He said to his friend, "People hear what they're tuned to hear."

Listening is the most neglected part of the communication process. There are lots of books and courses on writing and speaking, and we mention those skills frequently in evaluating the performance of employees, but how often do we consider listening skills? So much of the information we need to work productively and to make good decisions comes to us verbally. How much are we missing?

Types of listening run the gamut from what we do in an auditorium full of people to what we do one-on-one with another person. It includes formal presentations and chitchat in the hall. It's an important facet of our work, our family lives, and our social lives.

Why don't we listen better? Sometimes we're preoccupied, something takes our attention away from what's being said, or we're thinking about what we want to say next. Perhaps we want to talk rather than listen so we'll be the center of attention, or we think we already know all we need to know about what's being said. Maybe we think what we have to say is more important than anything someone else might have to say. Perhaps it's hard to hear or to understand the words. Sometimes we're just tired.

Occasionally it's something about the speaker, like an accent, monotonous tone, or distracting appearance, or the subject is complex or unfamiliar. The talk may not be well organized. When any of these factors are at play, we need to work harder to be effective listeners. We need to overcome these barriers to effective listening.

The New York Telephone Company, for some reason,

conducted a study to find out the most frequently used word in phone conversations. The word was the personal pronoun "I." It was used 3990 times in 500 phone conversations[9]. That raises two important questions: How well are we listening to others when we're talking about ourselves that much? How can we focus on others when we're that preoccupied with ourselves?

The real problem with poor listening is that the opportunity to re-listen doesn't come back (very few things we hear are recorded). If we do a haphazard job of reading something and later want to know more, we can read it again more carefully, but if we don't listen to someone well, we can never recapture what we've missed.

Stuart Chase[10] describes two kinds of listening. There's "sympathetic listening," in which we strive to ensure that we grasp the speaker's full meaning; then there's "critical listening," in which we look for motives behind the words, try to separate facts from inferences, and discover things about the speaker. Our minds certainly need to be in high gear when we're really listening.

We need to watch out for "selective listening,"—just hearing the part we like or that supports the conclusion we've jumped to. Shortly after we were married, I told my wife that I thought TV dinners were O.K., sometimes even good. You can be sure she heard that comment and reminded me of it on numerous occasions. We all filter what we hear, but we must be very aware of that process and use it very carefully.

You've probably heard the term *active listening*. Active listening means taking positive actions to ensure that we receive the speaker's message. It may include focusing on key words and even mentally organizing or outlining the material. A minister of a church I once attended always had three points in his sermons. He told you that there were three points, so you listened for them and it wasn't hard to remember them. He probably chose three, thinking that most people could remember three items. But remembering even three items requires effort on the listener's part. Active listening requires work.

In some situations you can jot down a few notes to help you recall the main points, but if you can't write any notes during the talk, maybe you can make a few notes shortly afterward before you forget things.

The step beyond active listening is *interactive listening*. This involves interacting with the speaker to ensure that we're receiving the message correctly. It's possible in one-on-one conversation or very small groups. We can ask questions when the message is unclear or incomplete, or verify that we've received the message correctly. These techniques are most important when the communication is important, e.g., when the risk of misunderstanding is high.

When listening interactively, we can make little responses, either oral or nonverbal, to show that we're listening and to encourage the person to keep talking. It also involves making periodic summary statements to which the speaker can reply to confirm our understanding of what we've heard. The summary statements may:

1. Check factual material.

Examples: "So you actually submitted the report on time."

"It sounds like you didn't know there was a problem."

2. Extend or generalize the material.

Examples: "You evidently went to great lengths to avoid upsetting him."

"You've done a number of things to improve the situation."

3. Focus on the feelings behind what was said.

Examples: "You must be very proud."

"That must be very frustrating for you."

Be careful not to put words in his mouth; just check your understanding of what he's saying. If he doesn't agree with your summary statement, try another one or ask some questions to clarify your understanding.

Interactive listening is advocated as a technique for interviewing, but it's helpful in all sorts of communications. It takes effort, but it works.

Good listening skills pay off in both our professional and personal lives. Listening enables us to learn, to understand others, and to show others that we care about them. Listening is the most basic component of focusing on others.

A boy was four years old and still hadn't spoken a word. Of course, his parents were worried about him and had tried everything they could think of to get him to talk. One night during dinner the boy suddenly said, "These beans taste terrible!"

His parents were shocked. His father said, "Why haven't you said anything before this?"

The boy replied, "Up until now everything has been okay."

Interacting with "quiet" people can be a challenge. I'm generally a quiet person. A quiet person doesn't talk much—that's all there is to it. The important thing to consider when dealing with a quiet person is how you can get him to open up. The first key is to try to understand why he's so quiet, and the second key is to make him feel comfortable about talking.

Have you ever thought about why a person might be quiet? What kind of experiences might tend to make someone hesitant to speak up, particularly to express an opinion? Maybe too many of his comments have been met with ridicule, criticism, or one-upmanship. Maybe too many times a comment has led to a batch of questions he couldn't or didn't want to answer. With quiet people, we need to be particularly careful to avoid such responses.

Never let on that you think he's quiet. That's deadly. Pretend you don't notice. Ask him an easy question or find a natural way to draw him into conversation. Then hang on his every word, and show him that you are glad to hear what he had to say. Be careful not to shut him down.

You may be thinking, "Why should I go to so much trouble to get this guy to talk? If he doesn't want to talk, to heck with him." But he may have something valuable to say and you may enjoy talking with him once he gets going. It's rewarding to help someone, and you're missing out on a resource if you ignore him.

You may appreciate these quotations.

"Quiet people aren't the only ones who don't say much."

"It is better to keep your mouth shut and let people think you are stupid than to open it and remove all doubt."

It's very important to distinguish between someone who is "quiet," someone who's "shy," and someone who's an "introvert." A quiet person is one who doesn't talk much, for whatever reason. He may not enjoy or know much about the topic being discussed. He may be tired or preoccupied with other thoughts.

A shy person is unsure of himself or lacks self-esteem, and this can manifest itself in quiet behavior. On the other hand, some people with low self-esteem are boisterous or talk incessantly. When you recognize that the person is unsure of himself, at least in the current situation, you can do something about that. Find a way to make him more comfortable, possibly compliment him on something.

Diana Spencer was, at the time marriage transformed her into the Princess of Wales, described as a shy person. She was called "Shy Di," but consider what she did in the sixteen years

116

between that time and her tragic death. She was one of the world's most glamorous and attention-getting women, who brought a warmth and "humanity" the British people had never seen in their leaders and who worked for the benefit of the less fortunate of the world. The worldwide phenomenon that occurred when she died demonstrated that she was one of the most widely regarded persons of all time. If that's "shy," then bring on all the shy people you can find. Our world certainly needs them.

An introvert is a person who is not interested in other people. An introvert can be shy and/or quiet, or he may talk endlessly, possibly about himself, while having no interest in others. Again, if you recognize introversion, you can strive to deal with it. But note that a quiet person is not necessarily shy, and a shy person is not necessarily an introvert. Some quiet people have a great deal of interest in other people. They may even be quiet because they do so much listening and observing.

Labeling people is always dangerous, and mislabeling them can lead to the wrong approach with them, and even if you decide on what you think is the correct label, keep it to yourself. Let others approach him in their own way, unencumbered by your opinions.

LISTEN CAREFULLY TO OTHERS, AND LET THEM KNOW YOU'RE LISTENING. — Key 2

Nancy runs an unusual "service." She runs a daily ad in the personals section of the local paper saying something like, "If you're lonely or have a problem, call me and we'll talk." Sometimes the ads mention that she's in a wheelchair and home most of the time. In fact, she spends most of the day on the phone as a "listening post." She gets at least thirty calls a day. Consider that, in her community, at least thirty times a day someone wants someone else to just listen. Depending on the situation, sometimes Nancy will tell the caller why she's in the wheelchair. It's the result of a failed suicide attempt, a jump that was intended to kill her but just paralyzed her. She says that before that she had a crippled soul but a healthy body. Now she has a healthy soul but a crippled body, and the cause of her healthy soul is *listening*.

Karla was a girl I knew in college. We had a couple of dates and on our first date we went to a movie. I remember how much I enjoyed talking with her on the way to and from the movie. I had a great time. But afterwards I thought, "How much more do I know about Karla now than I did before our date?" The answer was, "Very little." But we did so much talking, why didn't I learn more about her? I began to reconstruct our conversation, and then understood that she'd asked lots of questions and kept me talking about my favorite subject—myself. She learned all about me, but I learned very little about her. I was embarrassed. She'd outdone me. Ever since, I've been a much better listener and a much better observer of other people.

ASKING QUESTIONS

A few blocks from where I work is a small house with a sign out front advertising fortune telling, palm reading, and card reading. One of my co-workers was curious enough to stop in. Inside he saw a sign which read: "Three questions answered for $10." He asked the lady, "Isn't ten dollars kind of steep for three questions?"

She replied, "Yes, it is. What are your other two questions?"

Questions are important. In our interactions with others, questions are an important means of obtaining information and showing interest. However, there are some pitfalls:

1. Never ask a question unless you're prepared for, and can handle, whatever answer you get. Don't leave the person wondering, "So why did you ask?"

2. Never ask a question and then criticize or ridicule the answer. Ridiculing others is never wise, but it's particularly stupid after someone is kind enough to answer your question. Next time he won't give you an answer.

3. Don't ask for advice or opinions unless you intend to seriously consider them. If your mind's made up, don't ask for input.

4. Don't ask "loaded" questions. That is, don't ask a question if you already know the answer or if it's obvious what answer you want to hear. Don't force someone to lie to avoid hurting your feelings or having you make a scene.

5. Don't ask about things that are none of your business. Think about why you want to ask, and if it's not a good reason don't ask. Think about what you'll do with the information if you get it. If someone asks you about something inappropriate, don't tell him more than you really want him to know or more than he really needs to know.

The first three of these remind us that asking a question should commit us to sincerely listen to the answer.

In talking with others, especially quiet people, it's important to ask open-ended questions, i.e., questions that require an answer of some length rather than just "yes" or "no." Examples are:

"What do you enjoy most about your work on that committee?" compared to "Do you enjoy working on that committee?"

"What is the most challenging aspect of your work?" compared to "Is your work challenging?"

Some people will offer more than "yes" or "no" to a closed question, but others won't and you'll have to ask follow-up questions to learn more. The broader the question, the more information it provides.

Farmer Clyde was driving his truck and pulling his horse trailer when someone ran a stop sign and hit his truck, causing both the truck and trailer to flip on their sides. Some time later, Clyde decided he'd been hurt enough that he sued the driver. In court, the driver's lawyer asked Clyde, "Did you or did you not tell the police officer at the scene that you were fine?"

Clyde began, "Well, I had my old horse Bessie in the trailer…"

The lawyer interrupted, "We don't need details. Just answer the question."

The judge said, "That's okay, let's hear what he has to say."

Clyde continued, "I had my old horse Bessie in the trailer. When the truck and trailer flipped, I heard old Bessie moaning and groaning in the trailer and I knew she was hurt bad. But I was hurt, too, and couldn't get to her. Then this patrolman came up and looked in the trailer. When he saw how badly Bessie was hurt, he pulled out his gun and shot her between the eyes. Then he walked over to me. He was standing over me with his smoking gun in his hand, and he asked me, 'How are you?' I said, 'I'm fine.'"

We need to keep the answers we hear in context and strive to understand the feelings behind them.

We want our questions to provide useful information and to build rapport with others. We don't want them to weaken our relationships.

BE SURE THE QUESTIONS YOU ASK SERVE YOUR REAL OBJECTIVE, WHICH INCLUDES BUILDING RAPPORT. — Key 3

NON-VERBAL COMMUNICATION

Communication involves a lot more than just words. Sometimes how something is said is more important than the words. Tone, inflection, facial expression, and body position are all part of how a message is sent. For example, consider the following sentence. In each case, say it with the emphasis on the word in bold type. Notice how the meaning changes.

I didn't say he took your watch.
I **didn't** say he took your watch.
I didn't **say** he took your watch.
I didn't say **he** took your watch.
I didn't say he **took** your watch.
I didn't say he took **your** watch.
I didn't say he took your **watch.**

It's not just what we say but how we say it.

Consider the phrase, "I don't think so." If you say it without emphasizing any word, it just means, "I think that may not be the case." But there's a way you can emphasize the word "think" such that the phrase means, "No way!" It is much more emphatic.

Consider the phrase, "Excuse me?" If you say it with no particular emphasis, it means, "I didn't hear you; would you repeat that?" But if you emphasize it just right it can mean, "That doesn't make sense."

In each of these examples, the second usage is a fairly recent development; ten years ago no one used them that way.

Non-verbal communication includes how something is said, body language, touching, and even how close we are to others. You're probably aware that Europeans generally stand closer to someone when talking to him than North Americans do, which can make someone who is not used to it a bit uncomfortable.

The body-language business can be amusing, but it really

is an important part of the communication process. It includes eye contact, gestures, and posture. Watch people's facial expressions and body positions for clues about how they're feeling. Sometimes the body language even conflicts with the words. If we tell someone that we just want to have an informal chat about something, but we say it in a stern tone while sitting stiff as a board, we're sending them conflicting messages.

The flip side of this is to use body language effectively yourself. Be sure you're giving the kind of signals you intend and are not unintentionally putting people off. Recognize that leaning back with your arms folded across your chest is a "stand-off-ish" position, which puts a little separation between you and the other person. Standing with your hands on your hips often indicates impatience or disappointment with someone. Doing something else while someone is talking to you indicates that the conversation is unimportant to you (some would say it's rude). If it's a situation in which you want to give these messages, fine, but don't do them when you're trying to build rapport.

I saw a video in which a man was talking to a "big boss" as the boss was walking down a hallway, and the man was actually walking backwards to get in his comments as the boss was walking. Can you imagine how subordinate a person must feel to be willing to walk backwards to talk to someone? Can you imagine how superior someone must feel to keep walking and force the other person to walk backwards in order to give his message?

Leaning forward slightly, smiling, and nodding are non-verbal signs that put people at ease.

You can improve your appreciation of non-verbal communication by watching people converse when you're too far away to hear them or when they're speaking a language you don't know. Watching a conversation on TV with the sound off is also a helpful exercise. Try to figure out what's going on.

When my wife and I went on our honeymoon, on the very first flight a stewardess asked us, "Are you on your honeymoon?"

My wife later asked me, "How did she know that?" Maybe it wasn't hard to tell.

Watch the faces and postures of people sitting around a meeting table or standing around at a party. Increase your awareness. Develop skill in interpreting people's actions. Use that skill to your advantage, both in receiving and sending messages.

BE SURE THE NON-VERBAL MESSAGES YOU SEND FIT YOUR PURPOSE. — Key 4

INTERVIEWS

Interviews are a special type of one-on-one communication in which the objective is to obtain information and impressions. Examples are job interviews (offering a job or a particular assignment), exit interviews (when someone is leaving a job), and press release interviews. Whether you're the one doing the interviewing or the one being interviewed, most of the skills you need to be effective have already been discussed, particularly in the sections on listening and asking questions. I'll just make a few points specific to interviewing:

The *information flow* in different types of interviews varies. A job interview involves information flow in both directions. The interviewer must find out enough about the candidate to make a decision, and the candidate must find out enough about the job to make a decision, so each must strike an appropriate balance between talking and listening. An exit interview involves primarily a flow of information from the person leaving to the interviewer, so the interviewer must mostly listen, occasionally asking questions that will bring out the information he's looking for. A press release interview involves primarily a flow of information from the company representative to the media person, but the balance between information volunteered and that obtained through questions can vary widely, depending on the circumstances.

Both job and exit interviews require building rapport in order to get the other person talking freely. The interviewer's primary task is to listen carefully and subtly steer the conversation to obtain the information he's seeking. The exit interviewer must be careful not to put words in the person's mouth and just hear what he wants to hear about the person's reasons for leaving. Since the interviewer is still working for the company and probably likes it, he must be careful not to screen out what this person considered drawbacks to the company.

The following will tend to focus on job interviews, since these are generally the most challenging. Richard Fear has written a book[11] covering this topic in detail. He suggests that the candidate should do eighty five percent of the talking in a job interview, which presents a challenge for the interviewer. Very few interviewers let the candidate do that much of the talking. But listening carefully to what the candidate has to say is crucial to your decision about him.

Prepare adequately for the interview. For job interviews, review the person's files and list questions you have or matters you particularly want to discuss. Gather items (e.g., visual aids) you want to show him. You'll need to take some notes during the interview, but don't let it become a distraction. Write your summary immediately after the interview, before any impressions get cold.

In interviewing, it's important to ask those open-ended questions mentioned previously. For an interview, examples are:

"What did you enjoy most about your summer job?" compared to "Did you enjoy your summer job?"

"What was the most challenging aspect of your senior design course?" compared to "Was your senior design course challenging?"

The broader the question, the more evaluative information it provides. A broad question forces the candidate to organize his thoughts, and it is insightful to see how well he does that.

You've probably heard about "stress interviewing" in which the interviewer deliberately creates as stressful an environment as possible to see how the candidate responds. Maybe it's appropriate for some high-stress jobs, but not for the great majority of situations. The interviewer sets the atmosphere, generally very early in the interview, and an atmosphere in which the candidate is reasonably comfortable is usually best. (The candidate is under a certain amount of stress anyway.) That's not to say that the interviewer is to avoid stirring up the candidate; sometimes you have to ask some questions that make him uneasy in order to find out what you need to know. And you certainly need to ask some questions that require some thought, analysis, or generalization. I find it's insightful to ask about accomplishments he's most proud of or that he found most difficult. You might ask what aspect of his personality has been most important to his success.

You've probably heard of interviewers asking off-the-wall "questions" like, "Tell me a story" or "If you were a flower what kind would you be?" Seems much better to ask job-related questions. Candidates don't appreciate gimmicks, and I don't see how gimmicks provide relevant information.

As interviewers, we focus on evaluating the candidate,

but do we ever think about how he evaluates us? After one interview session, I was given a stack of forms the candidates had filled out which evaluated me as an interviewer. The forms included items such as:

Was attentive and responsive.

Appeared enthusiastic about the organization and what it has to offer.

Projected a friendly and positive attitude.

Made me feel at ease during the interview.

Provided ample time to present myself and to ask questions.

Was frank and honest with questions and answers.

This provides some valuable food for thought.

Be sure that the candidate is interviewed by a large and diverse enough group of persons. Gather input from everyone who has contact with the candidate, including a host who may not interview him formally but spends time with him. Some things come out better in less formal settings, like over dinner or when walking around. It's often better to get the interviewers and host together to discuss the candidate instead of relying solely on written input. But then beware of group-dynamic effects. Positive or negative comments can feed on each other in an upward or downward spiral that ignores the other side.

Remember that some people are better at interviewing for a job than at doing the job, whereas the reverse is true for other people. Strive to evaluate the candidate based on what's really important for doing the job.

If you're the interviewee, prepare by learning about the organization, organizing the key points you want to make about yourself, and planning some good questions. Prepare for questions you're likely to be asked. You'll almost certainly be asked about the types of experience you've enjoyed most, major accomplishments and contributions, and what kind of work you want to do. You may be asked the infamous "Tell me about yourself," so be prepared with a mental outline of key types of experience, traits, and interests you want to emphasize. Remember that you have to "sell" yourself. Have examples ready to demonstrate your accomplishments and strengths. Take some initiative in the interview. After you've answered a question, you can ask the interviewer a related question. That lets you get information you're interested in and makes the interview more of a conversation than an interrogation.

MEETINGS

Meetings are an important part of our communications process. A lot of manpower goes into a meeting, so it's important that we hold effective meetings. The following procedures will increase the effectiveness of meetings:

1. Consider whether a meeting is necessary and, if so, involve the right people.

If you don't have the right people, you may not be able to accomplish as much or you may have to have another meeting on the same topic.

2. Prior to the meeting, issue a written agenda that includes the purpose, proposed topics with time allocations, and attendees.

This will let people know what to expect and allow them to prepare. If you need specific pre-meeting preparation from someone, talk to him about it well in advance.

3. Designate a leader, scribe, and facilitator for the meeting.

The leader leads, the scribe records significant items, and the facilitator monitors the process of the meeting. The facilitator ensures that everyone participates and no one dominates, keeps the discussion focused on the topic (avoiding tangents), and keeps the meeting on schedule.

4. Start and end on time.

Don't reward latecomers, and be considerate of people's other commitments.

5. Capture ideas and topics that warrant further consideration (at another meeting) but that are outside the scope of this meeting.

Use a "parking lot," a place where you park (write) ideas to consider at another time. This will help avoid sidetracks.

6. Summarize key decisions and action items.

Follow up with a brief written summary if warranted.

7. Evaluate the effectiveness of the meeting.

Did you accomplish your objectives? Did you obtain everyone's input? What could you do next time to make it better?

8. Thank everyone for attending.

The facilitator doesn't have to be an expert on the meeting topic; he's focusing on the process. In fact, a non-expert can often facilitate better because he or she makes the experts explain unfamiliar topics, and because sometimes experts can be opinionated. Good facilitating requires practice and focus.

Even if you're not the facilitator, it's very interesting and insightful to watch the interactions among people in a meeting. Some people have a way of cutting others off, while others bring out the other participants. Some just seem to have to get in a comment every so often no matter what, while others don't speak unless spoken to. Sometimes a person will support or oppose a suggestion in return for prior reciprocal treatment by the person offering it. The outcome of a meeting often depends largely on the dynamics of the meeting and the personalities involved. When you're leading a meeting or concerned about its outcome, be aware of what's happening among the participants and adjust it as appropriate. Be sure you're getting everyone's input and that any consensus reached is truly a consensus and not a railroad job. People will support a plan, recommendation, or change, much better if they feel they truly had a say in it. Of course, they'll support it best if they feel like it was their idea (even if it wasn't).

Even the seating arrangement around a meeting table affects the interactions. We tend to interact most with those seated across the table from us. We tend to interact least with those seated right next to us. That's worth keeping in mind at the start of the meeting. Particularly if the meeting primarily involves a presentation, try to arrange for those who will be delivering most of the message to sit across from those who will be receiving it.

On the other hand, avoid having all the people from one organization sit on one side of the table and all those from the other organization on the other side. It tends to set up an "us-versus-them" mentality. That's particularly important if controversy or conflict is expected.

Teleconferences and videoconferences can let a number of people interact without travelling. A videoconference allows more interaction than a teleconference in that you can show items and see the people, although you often cannot see well enough to pick up subtle body language like facial expressions. A videoconference can be good for a presentation, but meetings requiring a high degree of interaction, like a brainstorming session, are best done face-to-face.

When you attend a meeting, strive to be an effective participant. That means:

1. Prepare for the meeting by reading the agenda and pre-

meeting materials, gathering materials you'll want, and thinking about what will be going on.

2. Be on time, and give the meeting your full attention. Maintain a positive, helpful attitude.

3. Participate in the discussion. Say what you think, encourage others to participate, and try to ensure that all viewpoints are expressed. Don't monopolize the conversation or offend others. Think before you speak. Make only relevant comments.

4. Be aware of the interactions, and help the facilitator keep the meeting on track and effective. Avoid distractions. Listen. Be prepared to summarize.

5. Be willing to take minutes if requested, and help with follow-up work. Share responsibility for the results.

MAKE THE MEETINGS YOU ARRANGE EFFECTIVE, AND BE AN EFFECTIVE PARTICIPANT IN EVERY MEETING YOU ATTEND. — Key 5

GIVING TALKS

Why are so many intelligent people such poor communicators? Sometimes it is because they never received good training in communications, either in school or on the job. Sometimes it is because they dislike this part of their job or accord it such low priority that they never devote much time to it. (Enjoying something and doing it well is a chicken and egg proposition; it is never clear which comes first.) Sometimes people doing complex work actually want their presentations to be incomprehensible because their objective is to impress people rather than to communicate. Speak and write to express, not to impress.

Effectively communicating complex subjects can

certainly be a challenge, but there is no subject too complex to be clearly communicated to others, even if they are only casually familiar with it. Improving your ability to write and speak in an informative and interesting manner requires some effort, but it benefits you, your readers and audiences, and your employer.

This section on giving talks and the next one on written communications are not long. There are books on these topics, and people who do these things as part of their jobs usually take courses on them (because their employers recognize the importance). But after reading books and taking courses, many people still have difficulty. I encourage you to take advantage of other resources. For example, many people find that Toastmasters groups do wonders for their speaking abilities.

If your job doesn't involve much in the way of giving speeches or writing documents, you may find it valuable, nonetheless. Your personal life probably involves occasional talking to groups and writing notes and letters. It's all part of your impact on others.

Some very important communication occurs through the talks you give. There are many instances when people, such as bosses, will take time to *hear* a talk on your work but would not take time to *read* a report on the work. Careful planning and organization, as well as clear, simple expressions are important in talks as well as in written communications.

In at least one important way, speaking is more challenging than writing. When someone reads something you've written, if it's not clear he can re-read it and study it. As a speaker, you have only one chance to get your message across. If a listener misses a point, it is gone forever (unless maybe it's retrieved during a question period at the end).

Your Audience

It's very important to analyze your audience before planning a talk. Ask yourself: What kind of background do these people have? Do they know much about this topic? What are their objectives in listening to your talk? What kind of speech are they expecting? What kind of mood will they be in? How will they react to your message? Will they be antagonistic? Will they have any hidden agendas? What is your objective with them? What impact would you like to have on them?

You must gear the talk to the audience. You can give a talk on nuclear physics to a kindergarten class or to a convention of physicists if you appropriately design these two talks.

WHETHER YOU'RE SPEAKING OR WRITING, THINK ABOUT WHAT YOUR AUDIENCE WANTS. — Key 6

Visual Aids

Visual aids can be a very effective way to keep your audience tuned in to what you're saying. People remember things they see and hear concurrently, much better than things they just hear. The most common visual aids are slides or transparencies (viewgraphs, or overheads) prepared in advance, and that's what we'll focus on here. In some cases, your audience is given copies of your visual aids, so that your visual aids become the documentation of what you said. People who didn't attend your talk will try to glean the essence of it by looking at those visual aids.

It's important to keep visual aids simple. They should let the eyes help the ears. They must be concise, easy to read and understand, and designed to drive home key ideas, usually just one idea on each visual.

You've seen speakers show a visual of a complex table or chart with fine print that no one has a chance of reading. Then he says, "I know you can't read this, but ...." Any time you start to use a figure or table you already have, like from a report you've written, as a visual for a talk, stop and evaluate it. It can almost always be improved, as a visual, by simplifying it.

Here are some tips for making good visuals:

1. Make two simple visuals instead of one complex one.

For a talk of a specified length, there's a trade-off between a larger number of simple visuals that you can go through faster, versus a smaller number of visuals that take more time because they have more on each of them. If you must use a fairly complex visual, find a way to build it up in stages.

2. Omit every line, number or word that will not contribute to rapid understanding.

For a list of items, use dots rather than numbers, unless you need to refer to the items by number. Tables and figures should contain only the items you will mention. Decide whether it's better to label curves directly or to use a legend. Remember that your audience will look at everything on the visual, and their minds will be trying to figure out everything that's there. Don't make them do extra work, and don't let them be distracted from what you want them to focus on.

3. Consider carefully the order in which you present things.

The order of things should never be arbitrary; there's always a best order for things. This includes the order in which you discuss topics and even the order of items in a list on a visual. It's even true when there are only two items. You often want to put the most important items first (for initial emphasis) or last (if that will help the audience remember them).

4. Choose the type of figure best suited to your purpose.

This usually means line graphs for showing trends, bar charts for comparing magnitudes, and pie charts for showing portions of a whole.

5. Put variety in your visuals.

Avoid too many all-word visuals, particularly too many of those in a row. Mix in some pictures, charts, drawings, etc., either putting these on one side of the words or interspersing them on separate visuals.

6. Use color effectively.

A variety of colors makes the visuals more appealing and can facilitate understanding. Think about appropriate colors and how to use colors to show relationships on the visual. Think about whether black and white copies will be made, and if so plan so that those copies will also be understandable (e.g., use different symbols on a graph in addition to different colors).

7. Get help on your visuals.

Discuss them with colleagues and professional illustrators.

Viewgraphs make a talk seem less formal than slides and provide more flexibility in that you can skip some visuals if you get pressed for time or based on audience reaction to what you've already presented. You can slip in a backup viewgraph, even without the audience knowing that you hadn't planned to use it. In contrast, once a slide is in the tray, you have to go through it in some way. But slides are required for some meetings, and they take less space when you're traveling. If there's a computer with a projector, you can use a file rather than physical copies of the visuals in which case it's like slides in that the file contains a fixed sequence of visuals. It's easy to hide slides in the file, but you have to do it before the presentation. The file is the most compact form for travel, but you need to be sure the computer with the appropriate software, and the projector, will be there. It's not so convenient if you have to carry those also.

Be sure you have all the necessary equipment for your visuals and that it works correctly. Make sure anything you need that you're not taking with you is really there. If you use slides, make sure they're in the tray correctly. If you use a computer and projector, make sure the two are compatible and set correctly (e.g., resolution). Make sure the computer is fast enough to keep up with you. In other words, test everything far enough in advance that you can correct problems. If you plan to use a computer, particularly if you're not taking all the equipment, a backup set of transparencies is a good idea just in case. Be prepared.

Storyboarding
Storyboarding is the process of putting your speech, or story, into a series of visual aids. You sketch and plan your visuals. Think in terms of a sequence of visual experiences for the audience. Plan how you'll use your visuals.

If you're projecting visuals, it's important to know if you'll need one projector or two. There will be some differences in the visuals if you can leave one up while showing a second. Plan which visuals will be shown on which projector. With either one or two projectors, plan to put visuals on and take them off at the proper time so that they don't distract. You don't want your audience looking at something unrelated to what you're saying at the moment. For a team presentation, you can have a storyboard review before the visuals are prepared.

Practice
A good talk requires practice. Practice the talk aloud

using your visuals. Practice in front of a mirror, if possible, or videotape it and watch yourself. Do a "dry run" to some colleagues or even your spouse. Don't hesitate to modify your visuals if you see ways to improve them. Time your practice speech to ensure that it is the correct length.

Almost all talks should be given extemporaneously from notes, rather than being read. Speaking, rather than reading, promotes better rapport with your audience and is generally more interesting to the audience. The President of the United States has to read most of his speeches because they set policy and must be carefully worded. You don't have that constraint. If you're required to write out a text for the speech, read it aloud a number of times to get familiar with it, then give the speech from notes. Having done that, you'll give it surprisingly close to what you wrote. Don't worry if it deviates a little. Don't take the text to the podium, as it may tempt you to read.

If someone is going to handle visuals for you, such as showing viewgraphs and perhaps pointing on them, be sure you practice with that person doing his role just as he will in the real thing.

Timing

The executive was scheduled to speak at a convention, so, as executives do, he asked one of his staff to write him a punchy, twenty-minute speech. When the exec returned from the convention, he was furious with that staff member. "Why did you write me a one-hour speech?" he demanded. "Half the audience walked out before I finished."

The staff member was baffled. "I wrote you a twenty-minute speech," he replied. "I also gave you the two extra copies you asked for."

Timing your talk is very important. It's the speaker's responsibility to give the talk within the allocated time. You've seen speakers with way too much material to present lamenting, "There isn't enough time ..." Baloney! You have the amount of time that's allocated. It's up to you to use it to convey the message you intend.

I attended a workshop in which several speakers gave speeches. The agenda was distributed, and it showed that twenty five minutes was allocated to each talk. In spite of that, one speaker, when he got up to speak, asked the leader, "How much time do I have?" Unnecessary question. Was he hoping to get more time? The leader replied, "thirty minutes," thus giving him five more minutes. I know he heard that, because he started by saying, "For the next thirty minutes we'll be discussing ...'. The man was wearing a watch (I later looked to be sure), and there was a clock on the wall visible from where he was standing as he talked, but he went on for fifty five minutes! That's inexcusable, inconsiderate, and unprofessional. It ruins your effectiveness in getting your message across. Your audience just focuses on how to shut you up.

PRACTICE A TALK MORE THAN YOU THINK IS NECESSARY, AND GET THE TIMING RIGHT.
– Key 7

Before the Talk

Visit the place where you'll give the talk. Examine the setting. Will you be sitting at a table with everyone else, sitting at a table on a stage, sitting beside a viewgraph projector in front, standing beside the viewgraph projector, standing at a podium, or standing beside a projection screen? Will you be able to move around? If you're going to stand beside a projector or screen, decide where you can stand so that you won't block anyone's view of the screen. These things affect the way you'll handle your notes and the way you'll point to things on your visuals.

I encountered an unusual setting at an after-dinner

speech I gave. I sat at the head table during dinner, and after dinner began my speech normally. But when I began using my slides, since the screen was set up in the back of the room, my audience turned around to look at the screen. I didn't see anything of them except the backs of their heads for the rest of the talk. I could have stripped naked while giving that talk and they wouldn't have noticed. It wasn't very much fun. I should have moved the screen to the front of the room before dinner.

Check the audiovisual equipment you'll use. Make sure you know how to operate everything. If you use slides, be sure they're loaded correctly. If you'll need to adjust the lights, know how to do it. Is there a microphone, or will you have to speak loudly enough to be heard without one?

Think about your appearance to the audience. Remember that they'll form an impression of you before you say your first word. You want to dress just a little more conservatively than your audience does. If people remember how you were dressed, you weren't dressed properly.

During the Talk

Speak clearly and with enthusiasm. Make sure the people in the back can hear you. Look at your audience as much as you can. Think of this as looking at individuals in your audience, not just the whole audience. Don't just take quick glances but make eye contact with individuals in the audience. Don't keep looking at the same individual, even if the audience is small. A videotape of a practice or real speech is good for improving this. At first you'll probably be surprised at how little you really look at your audience. Have a copy of your visuals so you can see them before the audience does and can lead into them. This will also help you to look at the audience rather than at the screen. Don't look at the screen. Don't keep looking down at the podium and hence showing your audience the top of your head.

They need to see your face.

Move around. Don't use a podium unless you have to, and even then don't stay behind it all the time. If you're using visuals via a computer, put down the mouse at times so you're not tethered like an animal on a leash. Don't stand where you block people's view of the visuals.

If you're given a laser pointer that jumps around to the point of distraction, don't use it. Trying to steady it with both hands is ridiculous. Carry a telescoping pointer with you just in case.

There is no topic that requires a dull talk. When the topic you're discussing is interesting, maybe even exciting, your presentation should be no less so.

Questions

Anticipate questions you may be asked and prepare for them. In your practice sessions, encourage co-workers to ask questions. Brainstorm questions. Have backup visuals when appropriate. If you get naive or unfriendly questions, be courteous. Avoid sarcasm, arguing, belligerence, or hostility. Don't be afraid to admit you don't know something. Focus on the positive, and strive for a good rapport with the audience.

Persuasion

Some speeches are clearly persuasive in nature. You're trying to convince someone to do something. But it's important to realize that every speech you give has a persuasive element. To be effective, you must win the confidence of your audience. Confidence is an emotion. You want them to believe you, i.e., you want to establish credibility. An objective of most speeches is to win support for ideas, work, program, work group, or yourself, so consider what kind of impression your speech will have on your audience. You may think that the speech is primarily informative, but there's always a lot more involved in a speech than information transfer.

WRITTEN COMMUNICATIONS

Your writing may include everything from one-page memos and letters to long reports. Some you write entirely yourself, while others include portions written by other people. The basic skills for effective writing are the same. You want to state your main ideas clearly and support them well. In the following, I'll use the term "report" for the written product, but remember it can be anything you write.

The Readers

A good report requires careful planning, and the first step in planning is to analyze your readers. Ask yourself: "Who will read this report?" and "What will they want to know?"

Of course, your reports will be read by people whose needs and interests differ widely. In general, however, your readers will fall into two categories:

1. Managers and others who will be primarily interested in your conclusions and recommendations, and

2. Those who will also need to know how you did your work and arrived at your conclusions (e.g., people who are doing similar work).

A report that gives the conclusions and recommendations first, then goes on to explain the details serves the needs of both. Even those readers who need the details would like to get the overall picture first.

When analyzing your readers, also ask yourself if there are personal aspects, such as matters of diplomacy and policy, associated with your report. Don't leave these to your supervisor, but rather face them squarely and decide how you will handle them.

By the way, I don't believe in "memos to file." People

shouldn't correspond with filing cabinets. You can always address it to your immediate leader or supervisor.

Your Purpose

The next step in planning is to determine the purpose of your report. What is your main message? If you were to meet one of your readers face-to-face, what would be the first thing you'd tell him? Jot down this basic message, and then add any subordinate ones.

Outline

Outlines are a tool to organize your report. For a large report, you may want to outline in two stages: first, a basic framework, then an expanded outline with more subheadings and detail. A logical, complete sequence is the important thing, not the form of the outline.

Organize your report so that it gets to the point quickly. State your ideas, decisions, conclusions, and requests before you give explanations, details, and substantiation. Put the more important things before less important things. Remember how newspaper articles are written. The who, what, where, when, and why are up front, followed by successively greater levels of detail. This way, the reader can stop at any point, depending on the level of detail he needs.

Note that this ordering usually reverses the sequence in which the work was done. When doing your work, you start with background information (related work), then develop methods, then produce results, and finally derive conclusions. Your report, however, should start at the other end.

Go over your outline repeatedly and critically, and keep revising until you are satisfied that it meets your goals. It is at the outline stage that the big errors are made that later require major revisions. Get suggestions on the outline from colleagues and your supervisor, if appropriate. It is much easier to revise an outline than a report.

Getting Started

A good outline makes the actual writing much easier. However, if you have trouble getting started, you might begin with one of the easier sections. Don't feel that you have to start at the beginning.

If your report is very long, it should begin with a summary, which is best written last. In some reports, a brief introduction may precede the summary, just to put the work into perspective. However, if you do this you must minimize this introduction. It shouldn't be longer than a paragraph or two. Don't make the reader wait to get at that summary. An introductory paragraph at the beginning of the summary is preferable to a separate introduction section. More background can be given after the summary.

If you have tables and figures, prepare them first and put them in order. Then write the discussion for each of them. This can help you get started if you're having difficulty.

WORK HARD TO MAKE YOUR WRITING AS CLEAR AND CONCISE AS POSSIBLE. — Key 8

Be Clear and Concise

Search for the simpler word, phrase, and construction. Strive to write more like you talk (but avoid slang). It helps to read aloud what you've written.

Table 1 contains examples of writing I've found in actual reports, along with suggestions for simplifying and clarifying them. A few general comments on them follow.

Many people feel that a formal report must be impersonal, hence the passive voice is the standard construction for reports. When a writer gets into the passive-voice mode he tends to use it for everything, which adds unnecessary words and makes the writing less interesting. Table 1 shows several examples in which active voice can be used while remaining impersonal. Many organizations now allow a more conversational style, including the use of "I," or more commonly the editorial "we," in more and more documents. So before assuming you're doomed to using passive voice, look at some documents and ask some questions.

Some of the improper uses of "they" and "their" stem from a desire to be gender-neutral without using "one," which sounds stilted, or "his or her," which is awkward. The English language doesn't have the pronoun we're looking for here, since we don't use "it" for people. But don't misuse "they" or their," because a desire to be gender neutral doesn't justify incorrect grammar. Sometimes you can make the subject plural to match the "they" or "their." Sometimes you can replace "their" with "a."

Be sure that the reader will pick up the proper reference for a pronoun. This generally means placing the pronoun close enough to its antecedent. Also place a phrase close to what it refers to. Misplaced modifiers or phrases and ambiguous references lead to those humorous ads you may have seen, such as:

For sale: Antique desk suitable for lady with thick legs and large drawers.

Three-year old teacher needed for pre-school. Experience preferred.

Dog for sale. Will eat anything. Especially fond of children.

Auto repair service. Try us once, and you'll never go anywhere again.

Used cars. Why go elsewhere to be cheated? Come here first.

Note that references must be clear not only within a sentence but also between different sentences.

You may think that it can't be very important to save a few words. But simpler structure is much easier on your reader. You don't want the reader to have to work unnecessarily hard to understand your writing.

Some writers are concerned about repeating the same word too much, so they use synonyms, which makes the reading harder. The reader's mind has do extra work to figure out that you're referring to the same thing. For example, if you write:

We stored the extra parts in a large box. When the next group opened the container, they were baffled.

The reader must figure out that the "container" is the "box". I'm sure that doesn't seem too big a task, but if you keep making him figure out references like that throughout your writing he will find your writing more difficult than it has to be. Little things make the difference.

Cool, Then Revise and Edit

Don't be satisfied with your first draft. Any report can be improved considerably by a second pass. Professional writers, even novelists, revise extensively, and modern word processors are wonderful for revising and editing.

Schedule your writing so that you can put the first draft aside for a few days before starting to revise it. This cooling period will allow you to analyze your first draft more objectively, more like another person would do. Get others to review and comment on it.

Although revision is always necessary, the extent of it may vary widely, depending on the way you approach writing and what you're writing. Tradeoffs are possible between the time spent on the first draft and that spent revising.

The things you look for during the revision are the same that you tried to put into your first draft, namely, a logical flow of information, and clear, concise sentences. Your advantage at this point is that you've captured the thoughts, so now you can critically examine what you've written. You can focus on how the reader will respond to it. See it as your reader will see it. If something is unclear to you it will be unclear to your readers too. Effective revision requires that you overcome the attachment you usually come to feel for what you've written. When revising, you must be ruthless.

To allow lots of time for revision, you should start writing the report as early as possible. You can write much of the report before the work and the results are complete. Start writing the objective, background, and methodology as you're doing the work. If you wait until the work is complete to start writing, everyone will be in a hurry to see the report and you'll rush it. After doing careful work on the project, it's foolish to rush the report and allow its quality to suffer as a result, particularly since the report is the visible and lasting record of the work.

There are two other advantages to starting the writing process as early as possible: First, it helps you to be result-oriented and identify gaps in the work. If you have trouble explaining something, it may be a clue that you should do additional work in that area. If you're writing as you're doing the work, you can more easily extend the work. Second, having at least a partial draft makes it much easier if you get pulled off the job and someone else must complete it.

Use Informative Headings

Report headings can emphasize conclusions and help readers follow your thoughts. When revising, check to be sure that you're using headings effectively. Don't feel compelled to use "standard" headings like Summary, Introduction, Conclusions, and Recommendations. You can use informative headings that emphasize key points and show your readers where you're headed. Note that the headings in this section are like that.

You may feel that such headings are too informal for certain reports. If you can't make the major headings informative, why not the subheadings? Breaking up a long section into a series of shorter subsections with informative headings makes the report easier to follow. Also, if the table of contents includes the informative headings it provides a good index of the contents and facilitates finding things.

Insert Tables and Figures

Small, simple tables and figures set into the text are valuable for illustrating points without requiring readers to flip pages to find supporting data. Often you can put a complex table near the back of the report (or perhaps in an appendix), and then abstract some key data to illustrate points by means of an inset table. Inset tables and figures must be kept very simple.

Table 1—Examples of Writing Clearly

Eliminating passive voice:

"It was voiced on several occasions that... **versus** Several participants stated that...

It can be concluded that... **versus** This work supports the following conclusions:

It was determined that... **versus** The results showed that...

Improper or awkward references:

Everyone must show their badge. **versus** Everyone must show his/her badge.

Anyone who has a project they would like to consider... **versus** Anyone who has a project he/she would like to consider... *everyone and anyone are singular; common error.*

Such a task would require a large effort to keep updated. **versus** Updating this manual would require a large effort.

In the previous section, this was studied... **versus** As discussed in the previous section, this was studied...

The wall location was changed and was located... **versus** The wall was moved from...

Unnecessary words:

... is dependent upon ...	**vs.**	... depends on ...
The reason is because ...	**vs.**	The reason is ...
... large amount of effort ...	**vs.**	... large effort ...
... at a further distance from ...	**vs.**	... farther from ...
... results that were obtained ...	**vs.**	...results obtained ...

Using gerunds (-ing forms) to simplify:

...will involve measurement of... **vs.** ...will involve measuring...

...by the introduction of... **vs.** ...by introducing...

Ambiguous parts of speech:

...will enhance venting and therefore lower pressures... **vs.** ...will enhance venting and therefore decrease pressures...
(lower *can be an adjective or a verb*)

EXPRESSIONS

I have often thought that there are a lot of expressions

that may not be understood by everyone. The origin of some of them is very interesting. Many come from animals, mythology, fables, and sports. I've compiled some of them in the interest of clearer communications, and because they're sort of fun too. I'll give the expression, what it means, an example, and a bit of explanation about the origin, etc. I'm not sure I have all the answers on the explanations and origins, however.

Behind the eight ball—in a difficult situation
With no transportation available, I was really behind the eight ball.

In pool, you have to sink the eight ball last. If you knock it in before all the other balls are in you lose, so if the ball you're after is behind the eight ball you have a difficult shot.

Bird dog—to keep after something, keep checking on the progress
I have to keep bird-dogging him about the report.

Imagine the relentless way a hunting dog goes after a bird.

Bird in the hand—something coming to you that you're sure of
I wasn't sure about his offer, but it was a bird in the hand.

From the saying "a bird in the hand is worth two in the bush." One the hunter already has is better than two he might be able to get.

Bite the bullet—to take action on something unpleasant or unwelcome
I finally had to bite the bullet and replace my roof.

Lacking anesthetics in the Old West, people having surgery would bite down hard on a bullet to take their mind off the pain.

Both barrels—to provide an extra measure of corrective action
I let her have it with both barrels.
From the double-barreled shotgun.

Bottom of the barrel—the worst of the lot
They were scraping the bottom of the barrel when they staffed the project.
Some liquids stored in barrels contain sludge or solids that tend to settle to the bottom.

Brass Tacks—getting down to brass tacks means taking something seriously
After you sign the letter of intent, we'll get down to brass tacks.
In stores where cloth was sold by the yard, the measuring table used to have a set of brass tacks carefully located to ensure correct measurements.

Briar patch—a place you say you don't want to go so that you'll get to go there (and you really want to go there).
I told her I could go anywhere but Florida, so let's pack our swimsuit. The old "briar patch" routine is sure to work.
In the Uncle Remus fable, Brer' Rabbit pleaded with his captors not throw him into the briar patch, so that's just what they did. Rabbits love running around in briar patches.

Cat nap—a brief nap
I caught a cat nap on the way.
Cats, like many other animals, take a lot of short naps.

Chicken/chicken out—to be afraid to do something
I was going on the roller coaster, but at the last minute I chickened out.
I don't know, are chickens more afraid of things than other creatures?

Chicken and egg—not knowing which of two items came first

Liking something and being good at it is a chicken-and-egg situation.

From that classic question of whether the chicken or the egg came first.

Crawfish—to go back on a deal or reverse your position

When I reminded her of her promise, she started crawfishing.

Crawfish frequently crawl backwards.

Cry wolf—to get people alarmed needlessly, like when there's really no problem

The weatherman's predicting a freeze again, but he's cried wolf too many times.

In the fable, the boy called out "wolf" a number of times when there was no wolf just to get attention. Then when a wolf did appear and he cried "wolf" no one believed him and hence no one came to his aid.

Dog—something that doesn't function well

That software is a real dog.

Being fond of dogs, I don't understand this but maybe it relates to the next item.

Dogging it—taking it easy, slacking off

He's been dogging it on this job for years.

I guess some dogs, particularly older ones, take it pretty easy (but a lot of dogs certainly don't). In contrast is the expression "working like a dog."

Ducks in a row—to have all aspects of a situation under control

To make this sale, we'll need to have all of our ducks in a row.

This relates to the way baby ducks line up behind their mother when swimming, but it could also refer to the way ducks fly in a V pattern (consisting of two rows).

Eagle eye—a very sharp perception
She has an eagle eye for corruption.
Eagles have very sharp vision, e.g., the legendary swooping down from high altitude to grab a small prey on the ground.

Fox guarding the hen house—someone with a vested interest in a position where he can do harm
The club president was in charge of keeping order at the party. Talk about the fox guarding the hen house!
If you assigned a fox to guard a hen house, you can be sure you'd end up with fewer hens and a happy and full fox.

Gold brick—to avoid work, shirk, or loaf. A person who does these things. Something worthless that's passed off as valuable.
I thought he'd be a solid worker, but he's a gold bricker.
Some have painted a brick a gold color to try to pass it off as a bar of gold.

Herculean—having or requiring great size or strength
Cleaning the garage was a Herculean task.
The Greek figure Hercules was known for his strength.

Like a duck on a June bug—going after something with great intensity
If you screw it up I'll be on you like a duck on a June bug.

A June bug is a fat insect that I could imagine would be a real treat for a duck.

Like water off a duck's back—having no effect
I gave him my suggestions, but they ran off like water off a duck's back.
A duck's feathers contain an oil that makes them water-proof.

Lion's share—the larger part of the total (well over half)
She received the lion's share of the estate.
I don't know what creature is sharing something (probably food) with the lion, but I wouldn't think that other creature would be too greedy in that situation.

Monkey around—to fool around, do something frivolous or that doesn't accomplish much
I monkeyed around with the carburetor for a while but it still wouldn't start.
Monkeys seem to be very playful.

Pig in a poke—something you acquire without being able to evaluate it well
Since I couldn't go there in advance, I was buying a pig in a poke.
An old meaning of "poke" is a bag.

Quick like (as) a bunny—fast
The place was weird, so we got out of there quick as a bunny.
Rabbits are fast runners, but I think this actually refers to their reproductive process. When I was a kid we took our female rabbit to have it bred, and when I commented on how

fast that happened my mother said, "Now you know why they say 'quick like a bunny.'"

On a short leash—under careful control

It's a high profile case, so they're keeping her on a short leash.

When you walk your dog and need to control him well you keep the leash short so he's close to you.

Slam dunk—something easy, a sure thing

I've known him for years, so getting him to agree should be a slam dunk.

In basketball, the surest kind of shot is when one of those tall players gets a chance to slam the ball through the basket.

Sour grapes—acting like something you can't have is not valuable

Her comments about losing the race were just sour grapes.

From the Aesop fable about the fox that kept jumping up trying to get some grapes that were hanging just above his reach. When he finally gave up, he said, "They were probably sour anyway."

Tar baby—something that once you start you can't get away from

I thought it would be helpful to clean his room for him, but it's become a real tar baby.

From the Uncle Remus fable in which someone was given a doll made of tar, and once he touched it he couldn't get loose from it. The tar just kept spreading.

Touch base—to have a brief communication to ensure that all is in order

I'll touch base with you tomorrow about that.

Baseball players need to be careful to touch each base with a foot as they run the bases.

Weasel—to work your way out of a commitment. "Weasel words" are deliberately ambiguous to facilitate this.

She tried to weasel out of our date.

The weasel is a long, skinny animal capable of squeezing through small openings.

PART 3
LAGNIAPPE

LUCK

A well-known professional golfer was having a very good round in a tournament. On one of the last holes he sank a very long putt to take the lead. Afterwards, a reporter talking with him about the game said, "You sure were lucky on that putt."

The golfer replied, "Yes, and the more I practice the luckier I get."

Andrew Lloyd Webber is the most successful composer of our day, responsible for an ever-increasing number of record-breaking musical productions. I've particularly become aware of his role in the theatrical world on my trips to London, where he seems to dominate the theater district with his block-busters. He broke into the public eye with big successes at about the age of nineteen. Was he lucky to achieve such success while still so young? He started his musical training with piano lessons when he was only three, so although he may have been only nineteen years old when he hit it big, he had sixteen years of experience at that time. I'm sure he packed a lot of work into those sixteen years, as he has into the years since.

Our local high school recently had an outstanding baton twirler named Starr. She was a joy to watch during the half-time shows at the football games. Her senior year she won all sorts of competitions, including a big one in Japan. Was she lucky to do so well? The summer before her senior year she

155

practiced twirling the baton for eight hours every day. That's dedication.

A woman I know, Linda, has, among many other attributes, a great figure. Something anyone would notice. (I may be middle-aged and married, but I'm not blind or dead.) What has been particularly remarkable is that she has retained that figure while moving into her thirties and having three children. Is she lucky to look that way? She works out regularly at a health club, runs in the park and in her neighborhood, and even takes runs when on business trips. As soon as possible after the deliveries of those babies she began working out. She also said that prior to the Christmas holidays she always sheds a few extra pounds to compensate for what happens over the holidays. So that great figure is not a gift but the result of a lot of sweat, strain, and willpower.

I used to work with a woman named Kay who had a lot of friends. Everyone seemed to really like her. Is she lucky in that regard? One day while in the cafeteria at work I noticed her getting up from the table to leave. Between that time and the time she finally exited the cafeteria she must have stopped ten times to talk with someone. In some cases she'd stand by them for a moment and talk, in others she'd sit down by the person for a bit. These people didn't flag her down for conversation, it appeared to be Kay's initiative in every case. I thought, "No wonder she has so many friends. She really works at cultivating friendships."

What we call luck is most often not luck at all but the result of conscious effort. We make our own good luck. When my sons went off to college, I wrote each of them a somewhat philosophical letter. I ended by saying, "I'd say *good luck*, but we both know it's not a matter of luck. So I'll say *best wishes*."

The industrialist Charles Kettering said, "I believe in luck and plenty of it. The harder you work the more luck you have."

Houston is the center of the gymnastics center directed

by Bela Karolyi. He's a good friend of my son's former cross-country coach, both of them having come here from Romania. Karolyi has coached a number of young girls, including Mary Lou Retton, to Olympic fame. I read an article about his latest protege who is training for the next Olympics. She began gymnastics classes when she was four, began competing at age seven, and is now thirteen. She practices from 7:00 to 10:30 A.M., goes to school from 10:45 A.M. to 2:55 P.M., then practices again from 4:00 to 8:00 P.M. She's arranged a special school schedule to accommodate seven-and a half hours of practice every day. I'm sure the girls in whose footsteps she's following did similarly.

People talk a lot about things they want or would like to have; accomplishments they'd like to achieve, but what matters is what we're willing to do or to give up to get what we want. How badly do we want it? Maybe I'd like to be an Olympic champion, but am I willing to practice seven-and a half hours a day for many years to achieve that? Maybe I'd like to run an immensely successful business, but am I willing to immerse myself in it, work long hours, take financial risks, and handle all the stress to achieve that?

This matter of making your own luck applies to bad luck as well as good luck. Making bad luck seems to come from the "It don't matter" syndrome (I guess the incorrect grammar "don't" matter either). I remember that expression from a scout in a troop for which I was Scoutmaster at the time. The scout was conducting a flag ceremony, and was carelessly allowing the flag to drag on the floor. Another scout pointed out that you're not supposed to do that. He replied, "It don't matter." Since then I've thought about things that matter and those that don't.

When Donald was a young man he thought it wouldn't matter if he used marijuana. So many others were doing it. He had no idea then that someday he'd be nominated for a prestigious position and that his use of marijuana would prevent him from obtaining that position. So it did matter, after all.

When John was in college he thought it wouldn't matter if he engaged in a bit of plagiarism to get through some tough spots. Certainly others had done it. He had no idea that many years later that plagiarism incident would rear its ugly head to thwart one of his ambitions. It mattered.

A real example of making both good and bad luck for oneself comes from the most famous alumnus of my high school, Pete Rose. He was a contemporary of mine. I don't remember knowing him directly but I certainly knew of him. He was the star of our school's baseball team. When he became a major league baseball star, those who should know said that he really didn't have as much natural talent as a lot of players but he made up for that by hard work. That's why he was nicknamed "Charley Hustle." Probably his most noteworthy achievement was setting the record for the most hits in baseball (4,256). Was he just lucky to become an outstanding professional athlete? Not really.

But then Pete got involved in gambling, and betting on his own team forced his dismissal from the game he loved so much. As if that weren't enough, some of his winnings evidently didn't get reported to the IRS, and that landed him in prison. It was ironic that his team won the World Series the year after he went to prison.

Excellence is the result of good luck we make for ourselves. Excellence can be an individual thing, as in the examples I've cited. Excellence can also be a group accomplishment. Certain schools, universities, companies, and other organizations are known as tops in their field. They are the source of great accomplishments. An example is the Bell Laboratories in New Jersey, where the transistor and countless other wonders have been developed. Juilliard School for the performing arts in New York is another. They are the places where the really ambitious ones in a field would love to work or study, but few are accepted. These organizations consistently have the top people, the "cream of the crop," and can continue to be very selective. Are these organizations lucky to have such status? No. They have achieved this level of excellence through the diligent efforts of a large number of people over a long time.

Are the people in these top-notch organizations lucky to be there? No, they have worked their way into them by years of hard work and dedication. Being part of such an organization is rewarding, because it is wonderful to associate with the best in one's field. Working with the best spurs them on to even greater accomplishments, but these people make sacrifices. They work very hard. The competition is obviously very tough because everyone there is a top-notch individual. Most of them will not, in that environment, appear as so much a "star" as they would be in a more common organization. It's a price they pay to achieve excellence.

I'm reminded of a young man who was on the high school cross-country and track teams with our son. He was a superb runner, who set records in junior high school and was clearly the star of the freshman teams. But did he get to win all those freshman races and look like a star? No, they needed him on the varsity team so they moved him up to run with boys three years older than himself. He did well, but of course he couldn't be a star among the older boys. He gave up some personal glory for the benefit of his team and to get better training for his later years. Of course, by his final years of high school he was a star on the varsity teams. By then he had paid some of the price of excellence.

Sometimes we feel a bit jealous of those for whom everything seems to go so well and we feel a bit sorry for ourselves for getting some bad breaks. We can get into the "Charlie Brown mentality." That is, "Why is everybody always pickin' on me?" We need to be honest with ourselves about what causes most of the good luck and the bad luck. Excellence is the product of self-made good luck.

BUSINESS

Henry just celebrated his fifteenth birthday, but what he was really looking forward to at this point was his sixteenth birthday. That's when a whole new world would open up for him—the world of cars. Like most fifteen-year-old boys, Henry knew a lot about cars, at least the sportier models that boys want to drive. He knew which manufacturer made which models, which ones were really performance cars and which just emphasized appearance, what kinds of engines they had, etc. The main reason he wanted to make some money was so he could buy a Porsche.

A fifteen-year-old is somewhat limited when it comes to jobs. He has to be sixteen for most of the jobs in the grocery stores and hamburger joints; besides, since he's not driving yet it's difficult to get to and from a place of work. But one thing a fifteen-year-old can do is lawn care. A number of his friends made money cutting grass. He knew the going rate was twenty dollars for a lawn job, including cutting, edging, cleaning up and bagging. He figured he could get enough customers near home to do about six lawns per week, at least during the peak season. Six times twenty dollars is $120 per week profit. Wow! That's a whole lot more than the kids who sack groceries or serve hamburgers make. He was excited. He could picture himself pulling into the school parking lot in that Porsche, and all the kids drooling over it. But Henry didn't know as much about "profit" as he did about sports cars.

The equipment was no problem, it was right in the garage, but when he mentioned the idea to Dad, he got a strange response. Dad said, "I paid four hundred bucks for that mower, and I don't want you beating it up cutting lawns all over the neighborhood." But then he became a little more rational. He told Henry he could pay his share of the depreciation cost for the equipment they had or else he could buy his own equipment. Dad said he might agree to a loan, at the going interest rate, if Henry chose to buy equipment.

"Four hundred bucks for a mower, huh?" asked Henry.

"Well, that's what I paid a few years ago, but now I've noticed that the same model is $460. When you figure depreciation you have to use the replacement cost. Actually, it will cost even more when we need to replace it, but the theory is that if we put that depreciation money in something like a savings account the interest might keep up with the inflation. So you can figure depreciation using current costs."

They added up the replacement costs. It was $460 for the mower, two hundred dollars for the edger, sixty dollars for the string trimmer, fifty dollars for the blower (it's easier than sweeping), and twenty dollars for extension cords. That's $790 worth of equipment. Henry decided to use the equipment they had.

They figured out the depreciation. Henry planned on six jobs per week during the peak season, but considering the off-season they estimated about 220 jobs per year. With all that usage, they figured the equipment would be shot in about six years. Based on that, the depreciation cost came out to sixty cents per job.

Then they estimated the other operating costs. The total for gas, oil, equipment maintenance, and bags was seventy cents per job. Well, at twenty dollars per job, that left eighteen dollars and seventy cents profit. Pretty good. Henry quickly multiplied that by the 220 jobs per year to come up with $4114 per year. Wow!

Henry started lining up customers. He was going to run an ad in the subdivision newsletter, but when he found out they charged for that he decided to just go around to some houses. Knowing that the going rate was twenty dollars, he thought he'd try for twenty three dollars in order to squeeze out a little more profit. However, he found that no one would pay twenty three dollars when there were other kids around charging twenty dollars.

Dad said, "Why is it every kid charges the same thing, $20? Are you guys getting together and fixing prices?"

"Are you kidding?" Henry said. "Those are my competitors. We'd never agree on anything. It's just that you have to be competitive on prices if you want customers."

Dad said, "What about the guys who've been doing lawns for years? Can't they get more because of that experience?"

"It's the result that counts," Henry said. "If the job's no better, the price is the same." Dad's mind spun off to think about the raises people got where he worked, but some of the thoughts were a bit scary.

Then Dad thought of something else. "What about the college kids? Shouldn't they get more? I mean, they're trying to pay their way through college."

That one took a bit longer, but then it hit Henry. "We learned in school that when people are paid according to their need, that's Communism. In the free enterprise system people are paid according to what they produce. It's the result that counts." Dad was a bit embarrassed that he'd fallen into that one and had to be reminded by his kid.

Henry got the customers and began work. Things were going well, during the month of July, a strange thing happened. Most of the kids who did lawns went on vacations with their families. This was also the time of year when the grass grew the fastest. People were having a hard time finding someone to cut their lawns as often as they needed to be cut. In fact, they became a bit desperate. They started offering twenty five dollars to even thirty dollars for a lawn job. Henry started grabbing all the extra work he could handle.

Dad said, "Is this a conspiracy to raise prices and take advantage of a situation? Is it 'price gouging?'"

But Dad became more rational and talked with Henry about supply and demand. Supply was down and demand up, so prices went up.

In the fall, another strange thing happened. All the lawn-mowing kids were around because of school, and the grass was growing much more slowly now, not only because of the cooler weather but also because it wasn't raining much. People wouldn't pay more than fifteen dollars now, and the kids were desperate enough that they'd take it. Times were tough. Henry figured that supply was up and demand down, so prices went down.

The next spring when Henry's Dad picked up his tax form, he picked up a 1040-A form for Henry. Henry said, "What's this for?"

"It's so you can pay the tax on the money you made cutting grass," Dad replied.

"You mean I have to give some of my profit to the government? What a ripoff!"

Dad said, "You haven't gotten to the profit yet. What you've seen so far is just taxable income."

The tax on $4114 was $614, leaving a net income of $3500. "Now is that the profit?" Henry asked.

"First you'll have to deduct your pay. Then what's left is profit. I suggest you take the $3500 as your pay and let this be a non-profit venture."

Henry figured the lawn jobs had averaged about three hours each. With the jobs themselves plus the time he spent working on the equipment, taking it to and from the shop, getting gas and bags, and everything else, he'd spent about seven hundred hours on his job during the year. That worked out to $4.86 per hour. About the same as the kids made by sacking groceries or serving hamburgers, including tips.

"And I had to sweat away in the hot sun on a grubby job for my money," Henry said. "Maybe when I turn sixteen I'll get a job at the grocery or hamburger place. The only reason I made more money than those kids is that I worked more hours."

Henry probably learned the most important lesson of all, that success requires hard work.

We are so blessed in this country to be able to work in the greatest economic system ever devised, the free enterprise system. Why is it "free"? We're free to engage in any business we choose to try, and to make as much money as we can. In a free market, prices move up and down due to the natural effects of supply and demand. It's too bad so many of our people seem to misunderstand the system and not believe that it's really free market forces causing changes to occur. They keep looking for other causes.

Like Henry, many people misunderstand the term "profit." Polls indicate that most people think that major companies make something like twenty percent profit. The truth is, it's about five percent. For every dollar the company makes on sales, it spends ninety five cents on its operations, leaving only a nickel of profit. That's a very narrow margin of success. It's obvious that just a small change in either the income side or the expense side could easily wipe out that nickel. It happens. Companies risk huge amounts of money to try for that measly five percent.

Is "profit" a dirty word? Is it some kind of excess money the companies shouldn't be allowed to have? Well, what can a company do with its little five percent, if it's fortunate enough to make it? There are only two choices: First, the company can use some profit to pay dividends to its stockholders, if it is incorporated; or, second, the company can re-invest some profit in some new facilities or similarly expand its business. If the company repeatedly doesn't pay dividends, people won't keep the stock and the company will get into trouble. If the company doesn't do some re-investment, it probably will also get into trouble, so actually a company must usually split its little profit between the two uses. Both stockholder dividends and re-investment benefit our society. Neither is the least bit evil. We should be so thankful that most companies are able to make a little profit, as they are intended to.

Successful businesses are the backbone of our free enterprise system and our economy. We owe so much to them, we depend on them. Why is it that some people appear to be set upon punishing them? Maybe there's a tinge of jealousy at work here.

The anti-business sentiment is particularly aimed at the larger companies. There's this "deep pockets" mentality. Some people think it's somehow O.K. to cheat a large company, as if they'll never miss the money. They file fraudulent claims against large insurance companies. They sue large companies, figuring the judge or jury will favor the small enterprise; but a large company is really just a collection of small companies. Its income is high, but so are its expenses, and it must fight as hard for the elusive five percent as a small company.

We should be thankful for large companies (as well as for small ones). Some tasks are better done on a large scale. In some cases, economies of scale benefit us all through lower prices. Some tasks are so large that only a large company can possibly marshal the resources to accomplish them. When our government seeks a private firm to manage one of its research laboratories, that job cannot be done by a "mom and pop" company. If our country is to someday obtain clean gas and liquid fuels from our vast resources of coal and oil shale, it will require investments in the billions of dollars. Only the larger companies will be able to do that. We certainly don't want to kill the goose that lays the golden eggs.

We should believe in free market forces. Gasoline prices normally increase a little every summer. We know that people tend to drive more in the summer. Those prices increase as the natural result of supply and demand. Why do some people look for some kind of "conspiracy" or rip-off motives? Don't they understand? An unusually cold period in winter will cause heating oil prices to increase. An interruption in energy supplies due to an embargo or an accident will cause energy prices to increase. When it's over, they come back down. The markets work.

We need to remember that the markets move in response to expectations, not just reality. Prices reflect what buyers and sellers think is going to happen. When a shortage threatens, buyers concerned about their supply and sellers concerned about replacing what they're selling tend to raise prices. Sometimes that causes consumption to decrease and production to increase such that the anticipated shortage never materializes.

Supply and demand. It's why a rock star makes more money than I do.

Free enterprise. It means if I'm jealous of the rock star's earnings I can let my hair grow out, get some wild clothes, and start singing. It's great!

We're so fortunate to be able to participate in, support, and benefit from our wonderful free enterprise system. Let's strive to make the most of it.

HEALTH

I'm sure you've noticed, as I have, that when you get sick, like with a bad cold, it just consumes you for a while. During the time that you really feel terrible, you just can't think about anything except how badly you feel. You can't accomplish much of anything. With a cold, that really bad part may only last a day. When someone contracts a serious illness, all his priorities change immediately. Everything he was concerned about before is forgotten, and all he can focus on is getting well. Obviously, our health is very important to us.

If you're going to have the energy to be successful and make major contributions, you have to stay physically fit. Particularly in this country where the "good life" abounds, many people are overweight and out of shape. Recent surveys have found that over half, some say two-thirds, of American adults are overweight. It's epidemic, and it's tragic. We don't need surveys to tell us that. Sometime when you're "people watching" at some busy place, just consider the physical condition of the people passing by. Look at the shapes of their bodies. It's a revealing experience.

Many people don't seem to have a clue about what to do about their weight and physical condition. It's very simple:

1. *Eat less.*

2. *Exercise more.*

I know some of you are thinking, "This guy's over-simplifying. Some people are overweight because they have a glandular problem. Not everyone is a 'jock.'" See your doctor and find out if you're one of the one percent with a special problem. When I see a very fat person, I sometimes wonder, "What does his doctor tell him?" Does he say, "Maybe you should lose a few pounds?" For the other ninety nine percent, the only glands involved are the mouth and the brain. And there's no reason to feel singled out, because essentially everyone, particularly those over forty, needs to be vigilant in this area. Even good-looking jocks. Keeping fit means controlling your weight and keeping your circulatory system in good shape. That's it.

Let's focus on the "over forty" set. When you're over forty, you can't live like you did as a teen-ager. I still feel like I'm less than forty, but I've been over forty long enough to learn some things about getting along.

First, let's consider food. We need to discard three ideas, probably instilled in us primarily by our mothers (mothers seem to have an instinct about feeding their young):

Three meals a day
The balanced meal
The clean plate

The only time three meals a day is appropriate is when the first one is eaten before seven A.M. Otherwise, make it two— and "meal" isn't a good term, because only one of them should be a complete meal. So it's a light breakfast and lunch (or brunch, if you slept in), and a normal dinner.

We need to be hungry at times. If you eat whenever you're hungry, you're in trouble. Hunger comes and goes, and it helps you enjoy your meals more.

The goal is a balanced diet, not balanced meals. If you try to include in every meal all those food groups you learned about in school, you'll over eat. Each meal doesn't have to be balanced, just your overall diet.

I have this problem with the "clean plate club." Remember Mom's lesson about starving kids in India? I tend to eat everything that's put in front of me, which is dangerous. Better to waste food than to waste yourself.

This relates to another hazard. There's a "misery loves company" mentality in overweight people. We need to be careful we're eating what we want to or think we should, not what someone else wants us to eat.

I've found a good way to avoid snacking at night. Right after dinner I brush my teeth thoroughly and floss them. Now I'm not going to eat again before bed because then I'd have to clean my teeth all over again.

Someone surveyed a lot of people who are successful in controlling their weights. They found that most of these people have two weight values in their head. The first is what they consider their appropriate weight. The second is the maximum weight that they will not let themselves exceed. Do you know how far apart those two weights are? Generally five pounds. These people don't let their weight get away from them. That way they never have more than five pounds to lose. Good idea?

Watching our weight is not enough. We can't assume that we're doing fine if we maintain the same weight over the years (and most people would be thrilled to do that well). The weight can change its distribution in two unfortunate ways: First, the distribution of types of tissue can change. There's a tendency for muscle to be replaced with fat. Second, the distribution over our bodies can change. There's that tendency for mass to move from other parts of the body to areas around the waist. Perhaps you've noticed that. We should weigh less when in our forties than we did in our twenties. Sorry to have to bring that up.

Now let's consider exercise. The problem here is either laziness or a misunderstanding, and let's clear up the latter. There is data on how much exercise it takes to burn up a given number of calories. Combine that with data on how many calories various food items contain and one can get depressed. It may indicate that it takes hours of exercise to burn off one piece of pie, and who's going to do that? (but who's going to give up the pie?)

The good news is that these comparisons do not reflect

how exercise works. It's not the calories you burn up while exercising that is important, it's the calories you burn up when you're not exercising!

Aerobic exercise gets your heart beating fast. If you do that regularly, it increases your metabolism, which is the rate at which your body burns calories. The teaching is that you should do aerobic exercise for at least twenty minutes at least three times a week. If you fall a bit short of this goal, there are still benefits, so don't give up. Anyway, this regular aerobic exercise causes your body processes to speed up, so that you burn up calories faster all the time, not just when you're exercising, but even when you're sleeping. The benefit of exercise works for you twenty four hours a day.

Of course, exercise has benefits other than weight control (by calorie burning). It does wonders for your circulatory system, lungs, and muscles. It relieves stress. I read that it's even good for the brain. Maintaining good blood flow to the brain helps prevent "neurological deterioration" in later life. I'm not sure what that is, but I don't want it happening to me. Exercise makes you feel better, have more energy, and sleep better at night. It's ironic, but when people feel tired all the time it's usually not because they're doing too much physically, but rather because they're not doing enough.

Another important thing about your metabolism rate: Whereas exercise increases it, dieting decreases it. When you decrease the amount of food you eat, your body's natural defense mechanism goes to work. It says, "This guy's not feeding me as much, so I'd better conserve what I am getting." Your body processes slow down so that you burn calories more slowly. Oh no! That's why it's essential to combine exercise with dieting. People who diet without exercising complain that the less they eat the less they can eat. They get discouraged, and the weight "yo-yo" occurs. When you cut down on food, as you must, you must also exercise regularly to keep your metabolism rate high. Both are essential.

These changes in your metabolism rate relate to changes in your body makeup. When you cut down on calories, you lose weight, but it's both fat and muscle that you lose. Losing the fat is what you want, but losing muscle is undesirable. Muscle tissue is what burns up calories. With every little movement, your muscles burn up calories. When you lose muscle, it makes it that much harder for you to keep losing weight. Exercise builds up those calorie-burning muscles.

I'm sure you've heard about the "bad" cholesterol and the "good" cholesterol. Cholesterol moves in our blood with a carrier called lipoprotein. The "bad" cholesterol uses low-density lipoprotein (LDL) and builds up on the walls of arteries. We can reduce our LDL level by adjusting what we eat. The "good" cholesterol uses high-density lipoprotein (HDL), which carries harmful cholesterol away from the arteries and thus helps protect us from heart attacks and strokes. How can we increase our HDL level? By regular aerobic exercise— another reason we to combine exercise with diet considerations.

I run regularly for exercise because it's super aerobic exercise. Coaches and athletes in other sports recognize the value of running. Running is convenient and cheap. You can do it at a moment's notice with no equipment except a pair of shoes. I run late at night for several reasons. First, that's the coolest part of the day, and in Houston that's an important consideration for much of the year. Second, I can go to bed after I return. And third, no one sees me.

It's amazing how your body responds to exercise. The first time I went running (in the post-forties era), I had a route around the subdivision in mind but I thought, "I probably can't go that far the first time. I'll slow down and alternate some walking with the running when I need to." I was surprised that I made it just fine. The next day my muscles were sore, as I expected. The second day they were sorer. To get in three runs per week, that second day was the day I should take another run. I wondered how long it would be until I stopped getting sore. I made the second run, which felt a lot better than the first. By the time I made the third run, I was no longer sore and never got sore again so long as I ran regularly. In less than a week my body had adjusted from sedentary life to exercise so well that my muscles weren't even getting sore. I was amazed. It's like my body was craving exercise, saying, "It's about time you did this for me."

My son's high school cross-country team had a week-long "camp" every year. They'd stay at some place and train intensively. One year they went to Galveston Island and ran on the beach. The people sunning themselves on the beach watched with considerable interest as this group of young men ran by several times a day. As they ran by, one man looked them over and commented, "There's not a fat one in the bunch."

There are lots of ways to get exercise other than running. Swimming can be great, but very few people work as long and as hard at it as is required for a good aerobic workout. Slowly paddling around a pool doesn't do it. Tennis and racquetball are good choices. It's certainly good to use activities you enjoy, but these "fun" sports can probably only fill part of your needs, because you can't do them often enough. Also, unless you're very vigilant you probably won't get as vigorous a workout from them as you need.

Stairs can provide good exercise. A fellow I knew used to get in shape for skiing by repeatedly going up and down six flights of stairs at work.

Our daily routines can provide a lot of mild exercise,

particularly if we're alert for opportunities. We can help ourselves by deliberately parking farther away, walking briskly, taking stairs instead of elevators, and zestfully tackling the more active jobs around the house. Less "couch potato" time can't hurt either. We should increase our general activity level in these ways, since it's so easy.

I get a kick out of people who go to a health club to work out but complain if they have to park across a parking lot and walk over to the club. Or the ones who take the elevator all day and then go to the club to use the stair-climbing machine. Sometimes they complain about having to walk up to the second floor of the health club to do their leg workout.

After I'd been running a while, I joined a health club. Not a macho gym but one of these places with the carpet, neon lights, and saunas. On the first visit, the staff gave me the usual little test to ensure that I wouldn't have a heart attack there and sue them. They measure your heart rate at rest and after some mild exercise. When he found that my resting heart rate was only fifty eight beats per minute, the guy asked, "Do you run?" Almost every time a nurse checks my blood pressure (which also gives your pulse rate) she asks me if I run. Yes, exercise really does make a difference.

The health club was interesting. While working out on that equipment, you have plenty of opportunity for people watching. I saw some people there who obviously needed to be there in the worst way. At least they were making an effort, I thought. I saw some others who looked like the people in the ads for the health clubs. I thought, "If I looked like that I wouldn't spend my time here." Of course, the reason they looked like that was because they *did* spend their time there. In fact, the ones who looked the best were the ones I'd see practically every time I went.

The health club provided another example of how the

body responds to exercise. At first I'd struggle with only a relatively small amount of weights on the machine. As time went on, I was able to add more and more weights and still do more and more repetitions.

The health club was populated about equally by both men and women. Some women think exercise is for men. Women tend to be into dieting more than men. Both sexes share the weight control and conditioning problem. I don't think a woman's heart is much different from a man's, although men may tend to have heart attacks at a somewhat younger age than women.

I have to chuckle when I see those ads that claim you can eat what you want and still lose weight. There's another one that shows a man straining with some of that health club equipment as it claims that "painful exercise" is not necessary. They're appealing to our wish to get something for nothing. Sometimes exercise does get a little painful when you're trying to really do yourself some good, but I'm sure open-heart surgery is painful too. I don't want to find out.

Engineers like me are involved with equipment of various sorts, designing it, trying to make it work, etc. You could ask an engineer to design a pump that would pump a rather thick liquid, at a variety of rates, very quietly, continuously, for 100 years with no assistance from the outside, no maintenance, lubrication, replacement parts, or any of that. He'd laugh at you. It's impossible. No one has built a pump that can even come close to such performance.

But there's a pump in each of our bodies that does just that. Our hearts. Our bodies are miraculous, and the heart is one of the most miraculous parts. Certainly we owe it to that precious pump not to over-burden it with excessive body fat or clogged arteries. It's miraculous, but we can't expect it to overcome all obstacles we might impose on it.

That pump does require *some* maintenance. We need to maintain it by exercising it and at the same time flushing out those arteries. The heart is a muscle, and you know how muscles respond to exercise. We certainly have all the incentive we need to take care of it, because when it stops pumping you know what happens.

All cars look great and run great when they're new. But the real test of a car, and the care that it's had, is how it looks and runs after 120,000 miles.

Ralph was a neighbor of ours when I was a kid. He taught at Ohio State University long before I went there. Ralph enjoyed water skiing. When he was in his seventies, he was still water skiing. His children, who were in their fifties, told him he should stop that, saying he was too old for it. I don't know if he ever stopped skiing or not, but I hope not. As long as you keep active, you're never too old.

By the way, my neighbor's full name was Ralph Paffenbarger. It's interesting that I've cited him for what he did to keep fit, and he has the same name as the researcher at Stanford University who was one of the founders of the modern fitness "craze." (It's called a craze because more people are doing it than ten years ago, but it's still a pitifully small fraction of the population.) Stanford's Paffenbarger did research showing that people who exercised had fewer heart problems. He must have taken his results to heart (no pun intended), since when he was in his sixties he was running one hundred-mile endurance races. And his children tried to get him to stop, too.

When I lived in Baton Rouge, some of my co-workers played tennis on the courts at Louisiana State University. On Saturday mornings they'd see a foursome of white-haired men playing doubles. They were all over seventy, and had started teaching at LSU after retiring from industrial careers. They were very good players. The young folks said they wouldn't have wanted to play against any of them. I guess their only concession to their age was that they played doubles rather than singles, so they wouldn't have to run quite as much.

Exercise is like feeding a lion—the problem comes when you stop.

So that's it. We need to keep the calories down and the metabolism up. Simple, huh? Maybe it sounds like I'm on a soapbox. I'm just sharing my experience in the hope that it's helpful to others. I'm no Arnold Schwarzenegger and I'm not a physician. I'm just a guy trying to take care of the miraculous body God has given me.

GIVING BACK

A man retired from the ministry at a young age, moved to the country, and took up farming. He did keep one tie to his former occupation, however, in that he served as a visiting preacher for the small churches in the communities around where he lived. He would go around to these churches preaching whenever the church's pastor was unavailable. On these Sunday adventures he'd usually take his son, who was about ten years old. One Sunday he was invited to a church he hadn't gone to before. He and his son arrived at the church some time before the service was to start, and no one else was there yet. They went into the church, and in the vestibule noticed a box with a slot in the top, obviously some sort of collection box. The preacher reached into his pocket and found only one quarter. He put the quarter into the box.

Soon people started arriving, and when the time came he preached. After the service, one of the lay leaders walked with him to the rear of the church. When they arrived at the vestibule, the man took the collection box and said, "Preacher, it's the custom of our church when we have a visiting preacher to give him the contents of this offering." He opened the top of the box and presented it to the preacher. The preacher looked in the box and saw only the single quarter he had put in. He took the quarter, thanked the man, and headed out with his son. A short way from the church, his son said to him, "Gee, Dad, if you would have put more in you would have got more out."

It's that way with everything we do. The activities we put more of ourselves into are the ones we find most satisfying. If we join an organization but don't attend many of its functions or do much with it, it doesn't do much for us. If you're an officer of an organization, maybe you put in three times as much time as a person who just attends, but maybe you get ten times as much satisfaction from it. If so, that's a good investment.

A wealthy woman died and went to Heaven. St. Peter met her at the Pearly Gate and welcomed her. He said he'd show her to the house where she'd be living there. They got in the car and drove off. Near the Gate they went down a boulevard lined with magnificent mansions. The woman admired them and said, "These are like the one we had on Earth." St. Peter kept driving. They came to some other streets with large, beautiful homes. She said, "These are a lot like the home we lived in for many years." St. Peter kept driving. The streets became narrower, the lots smaller, and the homes smaller also. The woman had stopped smiling and actually looked a little concerned. As they passed some pretty little "matchbox" homes, she said, "These homes remind me of the little house my husband and I lived in when we were first married." St. Peter kept driving. The homes became even smaller, but most notably they became more rundown. They passed some really dilapidated places. The woman said, "I'm surprised you have places like this in Heaven." Finally, St. Peter stopped in front of a terribly junky shack and said, "This will be your home." The woman was shocked. She said, "I can't believe you expect me to live in this mess." St. Peter said, "You must not understand how we work the houses here. You see, we take all that you give during your earthly life, save it up for you, and use it to build your house. With what you sent, this is the best we could do."

Giving involves time, effort, and money; they're all important. And it's important to remember that when we give, we're actually giving back, since the time and money we have were given to us. We all have the same twenty four hours per day; although the number of days we spend on this Earth varies. We can do things because of the abilities we've been given. The money we have isn't directly given to us, we have to work for it. But we earn it with talents that were given to us. We have a responsibility to develop the abilities we've been given so that we can use them. A little plaque in our house says:

What you are is God's gift to you
What you make of yourself is your gift to God.

The more we've been given, the more we're expected to give back. Congressman Bill Archer says that we all need to "pay some rent on the space we occupy on this earth."

I've mentioned my running for exercise. I've noticed something interesting about running: When you first take off on a run it feels great. You're moving fast, and everything feels fine. But it doesn't take long at all, maybe just a couple hundred yards, before it stops feeling good and becomes just neutral, not good but not bad. Not too long after that it starts to feel bad, and it gets worse. You're out of breath and your legs are tired. You start thinking, "Maybe I shouldn't have tried this right now, I'm not up to it." You may start thinking, "Why am I doing this? I don't like this," or even, "Maybe I'd better stop and either walk a while or just go home."

I'm sure a lot of people who have tried running do stop at that point. It's certainly tempting to do so, but those who do don't know a secret. The secret is that right there is the worst part. If you keep going, sort of fight your way through the bad part, lo and behold, it starts feeling better. You're still breathing hard, of course, but you reach a steady breathing rhythm. You're legs are still tired because they're working hard, but they don't hurt anymore. They just keep going with the rhythm. If you had a pain in your side, that goes away. I won't get into a discussion of whether it feels good or not, but it feels different and it doesn't feel bad any more. It's exhilarating. You feel like you're really doing something. You feel like doing more (at least up to a point). And when you stop, you really feel good. You feel satisfied.

In that first stage, it feels good because it's no strain on you when you're fresh. It's also not doing you much good at that point. In the second stage, you're doing enough to hurt. In the third stage, you've gone beyond that hurt and on to the good part.

I've noticed a similar phenomenon in giving back. Again, this includes time, effort, and money. When we give just a little it doesn't hurt at all, we don't even notice it. We're really not doing anything significant. When we go beyond that, we come to the point where it hurts, as in "Give until it hurts." We may think, "I guess I'm doing too much, I'd better cut back." But if we press on through that stage we can go on to where it really gets rewarding.

When our oldest son first joined Cub Scouts, the Cubmaster of the pack was Bill. Bill's son, who was in the pack, at that time was his third and youngest child. Bill said that when his first two children were growing up he hadn't gotten involved in their activities. He had been one of those parents who let the others do everything. He actually felt a little proud that he'd been able to avoid all that. But when his last child arrived at that age when kids begin to get involved in group activities he suddenly realized that this was his last chance. So he grabbed it, became the Cubmaster and who knows what else, and was enjoying it immensely. Better late than never.

In the early days of our country, there was a real sense of community because everyone depended on each other in such a real way. Most everyone raised some crops, but they raised different crops. The people had specialties, like blacksmithing, caring for the animals, etc. They exchanged goods and services so everyone could get along.

In our modern society, there's still specialization but we're not so acutely aware of our dependence on others. That's at least partially due to the fact that we use money to purchase goods and services rather than directly bartering. But there are a lot of important "services" that money can't buy. These are provided by volunteers. In this network we still have a sense of community. In a subdivision or local area, one father, like Bill, heads the Cub Scout pack. A number of mothers serve as den leaders. Other mothers lead the Brownie and Girl Scout troops. Various parents coach the local sports teams, lead the Indian Guides/Princesses groups, organize the school parties, chaperone the high school dances, teach the Sunday School classes, host the children's parties, and on and on it goes. As our children participate in all this, we keep seeing the same children and parents at various activities, and we keep seeing the parents in different roles. We watch the other children grow up and into more advanced activities along with our own. We see that we really do live in a rather close-knit community and depend on each other's efforts to provide our children with the rich array of experiences we want for them. It's a form of sharing.

The town of Monticello, California was a beautiful little town located in a valley through which the Putah River ran. What was most remarkable about this town was that everything there was so beautifully maintained. The people had so much pride in their town that they kept everything immaculate. The homes and public buildings just sparkled, the lawns and gardens were carefully manicured, and flowers abounded. No trash was seen on the streets. Visitors to the town remarked about the neatness and cleanliness.

In the 1950's, water became scarce in Northern California as the area grew so much. The federal and county governments formed a plan to dam the river to create a reservoir in the valley. The town would have to be destroyed. The residents opposed but could not stop the plan. They were given three years to move out.

An unfortunate but understandable change took place in the attitudes of the residents. Interest in beautifying and maintaining the town ceased. Even picking up litter became a matter of no concern. The appearance of the town steadily degraded. Everything became run-down; many real eye sores developed. By the time the dam was to be built, the town was such a mess that it really needed to be destroyed. When people stop caring, things really go to pot.

Fortunately, there are a lot of people who do care. Our communities are full of them. I know some people who put a lot of time into volunteer organizations, and I admire them for that. In the Masons, there are men who devote four evenings a week to the various activities of that organization. The Masons do a lot of charitable projects and have a stated goal of "making good men better." These men obviously consider those projects and objectives worthy of a major commitment of their time.

The scoutmaster of one of our local scout troops lives close to me. He spends about four evenings a week on scout matters, basically to provide a quality scouting program to young men in our area. And what an impact he's having! There are many more.

You know, some of those individuals I've mentioned as devoting so much time to volunteer activities are people I greatly admire for certain personal qualities. I don't think that's a coincidence.

Leslie is a nine year-old-girl who was born with no arms. She came to Houston to be fitted soon with two high-tech, electric, artificial arms. All the Sunday School classes at our church collected money to help pay for Leslie's arms. Kids all over the country helped Leslie in this way. They'd seen her picture but had never met her, and they probably never will meet her. But they still wanted to help.

There's a small, quiet movement going on in this country you may not have heard about. It was started by Eugene Lang. Lang was concerned about the fact that so few kids from the inner city near him finished high school. He thought of all the challenges facing our world, and how ill-prepared these kids would be to help with those challenges. He thought of the problems that result when young people go out into the adult world without adequate education or training to support themselves. He talked with school administrators and teachers about his concerns. They, of course, shared those concerns.

In 1981 Lang was giving a graduation speech to a sixth-grade class at a public school in Harlem. He was talking about dreams and visions of the future, encouraging the students to stay in school and go on to college. But as he talked he realized that it just wasn't going to happen. The dropout rate in this district was very high. So Lang made an impromptu promise to that class of sixth graders. He told them that if they'd stay in school and graduate from high school with good enough grades to get into a state university, he would pay for four years of college for each of them. Can you imagine putting fifty two kids through college at the same time? Can you imagine doing that for a bunch of kids you don't even know? Of course Lang had some money, but I'm sure he could think of lots of other things to do with that money. He also arranged for tutoring and counseling for the students, a support system to back up his promise.

Based on the historical record for that school district, one would have expected only about twenty-five percent of the class to graduate from high school, and almost none to attend college. But forty-eight of those fifty-two students graduated from high school, and forty went on to college, which is an extraordinary achievement!

Lang's action led to establishment of the I Have a Dream Foundation in New York, which encourages such commitments. It was so named because Lang had been quoting Martin Luther King at the moment he decided to become a one-man scholarship fund. Under this program, a sponsor "adopts" a class of sixth graders and pledges to pay for six years of tutoring and four years of college for students who stay in school. The minimum cost to a donor is $250,000. Last I heard over one hundred people had made the commitment, helping about four thousand students in fifteen cities. The program is growing. Not all of them are super-rich, either. One man who did it said it was the scariest commitment he'd ever made, he didn't know how he'd pay for it, and he immediately began a savings and investment program to try to get ready. Amazing things happen when people care.

When people care about others, when they realize that they have been given something they can share, they want to give something back.

A woman I worked with mentioned how disappointed she was that her husband never (maybe rarely) gave her any gifts. It wasn't that she wanted the gifts themselves. She had a good job and enough money to buy all she needed herself. All she wanted was to know that he cared enough about her to take the time and go to the trouble to pick out something for her and give it to her, just because he wanted to please her. Just a demonstration of emotion, that's all. Some time later they were divorced.

Gifts of all sorts are important because of the message they convey.

Jim passed away shortly before Christmas. In fact, his funeral was four days before Christmas. The church was packed to overflowing, since he was a very popular and respected man. He and his wife, Karen, had two children, one then in high school and the other in junior high. At home after the funeral, the kids asked their mother if they could talk to her in private, so they went into a bedroom. They told her they were concerned because they knew their father hadn't bought her Christmas presents. He had been shopping with the kids and showed them some things he was thinking of buying her, but he didn't buy them then because he wanted his gifts to his wife to be a surprise for the kids too. He said he'd return to the store a few days later and buy some things for her. But they knew he hadn't gotten back to the store before he died, and they wanted her to have those gifts.

Karen told them, "Don't worry about that. He already gave me the greatest gift he could give, and he gave me that a long time ago and kept giving it to me until he died. It was the gift of himself."

At Christmas, birthdays, and anniversaries we search for

the perfect gift to give our loved ones, something that will really please them. But sometimes we overlook the greatest gift we can give them: some time together, to talk or laugh or have fun or share a memory or make a new one. A bit of ourselves.

TODAY

One good thing about going to work early and driving generally eastward at that time is that I get to see a lot of sunrises. Many of them are very pretty, and I appreciate them. It's a good way to start the day. Pretty sunsets are nice too. I particularly enjoy sunsets over the water, so I try to take them in whenever I can. And a sky full of stars on a clear night is worth a good look no matter where I am.

A day that starts with a pretty sunrise or ends with a pretty sunset can't be too bad. Whether or not they're pretty, and whether or not we see them, every day begins with a sunrise and ends with a sunset.

One thing I've noticed when flying is obvious but worth thinking about. No matter how crummy the weather is when the plane takes off, in just a few minutes it goes above the clouds and the weather up there is always beautiful. Above the clouds the sun always shines during the day and the stars always shine at night. No rain, sleet, or snow. It's always beautiful. I fly along for most of the trip in that mode. It's only during the final descent that the plane goes back through the clouds and I experience whatever kind of weather my destination is having.

The layer of the atmosphere that controls the weather we live in most of the time is really very thin. Beyond that thin layer it's always beautiful. Most of what bothers us in our daily lives is like a thin layer that can shield us from all the beauty that's there for us—beautiful scenery, flowers, music, and people. Among all our daily routines, surely we can take time to enjoy what's all around us.

One morning my wife commented on a homework assignment our son had been working on and that he was taking to school that day. She said, "I think it was due yesterday." I replied, "Well, he can't turn it in yesterday. He can turn it in today." A bit later I decided that I'd (accidentally) said something profound.

Today is what we have to work with right now, not yesterday or tomorrow. It's important to have pleasant memories and to learn from past experiences, but we don't want to live in the past. It's important to plan ahead and to have things to look forward to, but we don't want to be always waiting.

Today is a gift. That's why it's called "the present."

There was a time when my wife and I were dating or just married, I can't remember which, when we found ourselves saying "someday" quite often. I guess we had a lot to look forward to. It became a little joke with us and we kidded each other about saying "someday."

The credo of Alcoholics Anonymous uses the theme "just for today" to encourage people to achieve difficult goals by taking one day at a time. Abigail Van Buren ("Dear Abby") has adapted that theme to more general self-improvement goals in a New Year's column that she publishes every year. She says that we can accomplish a great deal by taking positive action just one day at a time. So just for today I will be happy, be agreeable, improve my mind, face reality, be unafraid, etc. Good advice, Abby.

A long time ago in a faraway land an area was besieged with a plague of frogs. Now a frog isn't a bad creature, but in this case the frogs were just everywhere. Inside the houses, everywhere people looked, everything was just covered with frogs. They couldn't eat, sleep, or do anything because of all those frogs hopping around and croaking. They couldn't kill enough to make a dent in their numbers. It was gross. The people were really suffering.

So the leader of this land went to the all-powerful being of the time and pleaded with him to take away the frogs, promising great favors in return. The all-powerful one asked him, "When shall I remove the frogs?"

The leader replied, "Tomorrow."

Now here's the question. Why in the world did he say "tomorrow"? Surely the all-powerful one could have removed them immediately. Why would he make his people needlessly suffer through one more day with the frogs?

But we sometimes do the same thing, don't we? At times we have things in our lives that are messed up and that we're not pleased with, things that we're doing that are causing problems for ourselves and those we care about, things that we should be doing that we're not. We know we could correct those problems, but we say, "tomorrow." Why do we suffer through one more day with the frogs?

By the way, that story is from the Bible (the Book of Exodus).

Near the center of a piece of farmland was a large boulder. The farmer always plowed around it. But one day his curiosity got the best of him and, sort of on a whim, he edged his tractor up to the rock to try giving it a shove. To his surprise, the rock moved quite easily. Although it was large around, it was quite thin and didn't weigh nearly as much as he had imagined. He was able to remove the rock from his field, He thought of all those years he had plowed around it and wondered why he'd waited so long to try to do something about it.

I know how these things can happen. I was recently

reminded of that story by something I did. The light on our garage door opener stopped working. This model isn't one with just a plain light bulb sticking out. This one has a "built-in" yellow plastic light all across one end. Somehow I got this idea that replacing that light would be a real pain. I'd have to hunt all over for a replacement, and if I found one it would be expensive. So I just left the light alone for a few months, and did without it.

Then when I was standing by it I noticed some screws on the yellow plastic, so I decided to take off whatever would come off just to see what kind of exotic light this was. It was just a plastic cover, and under it was two plain light bulbs. I had them replaced in a few minutes. Why had I been afraid to try?

We need to watch that tendency to procrastinate. We're the losers when we put off helping ourselves or doing those little things to make others feel better (and ourselves, too). We need to take the initiative on those things that make our lives more pleasant. We need to stop and smell the flowers, and we need to do it today. Tomorrow may be too late.

There's an organization called "Make Today Count," or MTC for short. It's a support group for people with terminal illnesses. It was founded by a man who had a terminal illness. When he first learned of his illness he became very bitter and negative. He moped around asking "Why me?" making himself and everyone around him miserable. Then one day he had a drastic attitude change. He decided that he wasn't dead yet and that he'd start making the most of every day he had left. That's when he founded MTC. "Make today count" is a great motto for all of us.

The following essay, "The Station," by Robert J. Hastings, has an important message for us. It has been popularized by Ann Landers, Reader's Digest, and Paul Harvey on ABC news.

"The Station"

Tucked away in our subconscious minds is an idyllic vision in which we see ourselves on a long journey that spans an entire continent. We are traveling by train and, from the windows, we drink in the passing scenes of cars on nearby highways, of children waving at crossings, of cattle grazing in distant pastures, of smoke pouring from power plants, of row upon row of cotton and corn and wheat, of flatlands and valleys, of city skylines and village halls.

But uppermost in our minds is our final destination—for at a certain hour and on a given day, our train will finally pull into the station with bells ringing, flags waving, and bands playing. And once that day comes, so many wonderful dreams will come true. So, restlessly we pace the aisles and count the miles, peering ahead, waiting, waiting, waiting for the station.

"Yes, when we reach the station, that will be it!" we promise ourselves. "When we're eighteen ... win that promotion ... put the last kid through college ... buy that 450 SL Mercedes Benz ... pay off the mortgage ... have a nest egg for retirement."

From that day on we will all live happily ever after.

Sooner or later, however, we must realize there is no station in this life, no one earthly place to arrive at once and for all. The journey is the joy. The station is an illusion—it constantly outdistances us. Yesterday's a memory, tomorrow's a dream. Yesterday belongs to history, tomorrow belongs to God. Yesterday's a fading sunset, tomorrow's a faint sunrise. Only today is there light enough to love and live.

So, gently close the door on yesterday and throw the key away. It isn't the burdens of today that drive men mad, but rather the regrets over yesterday and the fear of tomorrow.

So stop pacing the aisles and counting the miles. Instead, swim more rivers, climb more mountains, kiss more babies, count more stars. Laugh more and cry less. Go barefoot more often. Eat more ice cream. Ride more merry-go-rounds. Watch more sunsets. Life must be lived as we go along.

-by Robert J. Hastings

If there is a station, it's beyond this earthly life, and will come soon enough. Let's all strive to savor the moment, enjoy the "little things," stop putting things off, and dig in.

I've devised a method for helping us focus on moving forward from today. It's called "If I Died Today." Here's how it works. This is a bit gross, but just imagine for a moment, very hypothetically, that you died today. The person who knows you best at this time is asked to deliver the eulogy at your funeral. It isn't always clergy who do this. I attended a funeral for a friend, Betty, at which the most meaningful comments were by her husband. Her sons also spoke. It's difficult for loved ones to speak at such a time, but if they can muster up the courage it's very good because they know the deceased better than anyone else.

When someone gives a eulogy, he cuts out all the superfluous stuff and focuses on the really significant things about the deceased. The characteristics that really mattered. The accomplishments having long-term impact. The unforgettable things.

Think about what that loved one would say about you. What would he emphasize? What would he leave out?

Having thought about it, of course, the best thing to do next is to ask that person to write out the eulogy. He may think you've flipped at first, but hopefully you can talk him into it.

Then read it thoughtfully and discuss it with him. Maybe you're the appropriate one to write one for him in return. Then you can discuss both of them.

Eulogies usually recall certain events from the past to illustrate points about the person. They may go way back, and then bring things right up to the present. They may go on to speculate a bit about your life in the hereafter. Now there's where we have to draw a firm line. The person writing your eulogy must stop abruptly at today. He can't extend things for one minute. Because you did not die today, the story is not over! Only you can finish that story. You can finish it any way you like. And you'll do it one day at a time, starting today!

PURPOSE

I've mentioned my interest in boating. When we bought our first boat we didn't buy an anchor. It wasn't required at that time and place, and we didn't think we'd need one. When we'd stop for lunch on the lake, the boat would keep drifting into shore so that we'd have to keep re-starting the motor and moving it back out. When we'd stop for a swim, the boat would drift. When we tied it up on a beach, the back end would swing around with the waves. After learning that an anchor is useful, we bought one.

I've made three week-long sailing/snorkeling trips to the Florida Keys with groups of boys, including my sons. They were three of the most enjoyable weeks I've spent. Each trip was different, involving different-sized boats. The area is beautiful, and snorkeling on those colorful coral reefs alongside all the amazing tropical fish is fantastic.

It was on the first of these trips that I really learned the value of anchors. We stayed on two twenty five-foot sailboats.

During the days we sailed from place to place, snorkeled on the reefs and on a shipwreck, and even caught some lobsters. At night we'd pull into a bay, anchor, and sleep on the boats, which had cabins. The bays contained a number of boats at anchor, with people sleeping in some of them, I'm sure, so we had to be sure our boat wouldn't drift while we slept. Every night we'd put out two anchors attached to the bow, putting them at about a thirty-degree angle from each other. We'd stomp them into the bottom. Two anchors placed like that ensure that the boat doesn't drift or rotate. One evening there was a storm and we kept an "anchor watch." We took turns watching to be sure our anchors didn't give way. Near daybreak, one of the anchors did come loose and the boat started swaying, but we made it through the night.

On the third trip, we stayed on a forty-foot sailboat. We used a single anchor (let the boat swing), and had two people on anchor watch in two-hour shifts all night, every night. My son and I enjoyed some quiet time in the middle of the night. If you have to get up, or stay up, in the middle of the night to watch your anchors, they must be very important.

The hot air balloon was invented and used long before the first airplanes. Of course, some people enjoy riding them today, but the hot air balloon never has been a serious mode of transportation for one very important reason: You cannot direct them. You can control the altitude of the balloon, and thus catch different winds at different elevations, but you still basically go where the wind takes you. When people use hot air balloons for recreation, they have a "chase car" that follows the balloon. Drifting with the wind can be relaxing fun, but for transportation we need to be able to control where we go.

Drifting through life just won't do. We need to move with a purpose.

Even a dead log will float downstream. It takes energy to move upstream. Anyone can sail a boat with the wind, but a skilled sailor can use a given wind to go any direction he chooses. If you just coast, you can't go anywhere but downhill.

When I was a kid, my brother and I and some of our friends enjoyed spelunking, which means cave exploring. Spelunkers make fun of the commercial caves with walkways, stairs, handrails, and electric lights. They like wild caves, just as nature made them. You squeeze through tight passages, swim through fifty five-degree water, and crawl through mud. Great fun! My brother did it with various groups for many years, and gained some notoriety from it.

To find wild caves, you must drive around country roads a lot. On one adventure, we had twisted around enough that we were lost (but we wouldn't admit that). On one road we met a farmer so we stopped to ask directions. We asked, "Is this the road to Waynesville?"

He replied, "Yes it is." As we were pulling away, we barely heard him add, "But you're going the wrong way."

One item I've always carried in our boat is a compass, although we boat mostly on small inland waterways where you shouldn't need a compass. I recall using it only once. On an unfamiliar part of a lake, I was trying to get back to where I'd launched. I was going parallel to shore but wasn't sure I was going the right way, so I checked the compass and verified my route.

It was on that second trip to the Florida Keys that I really learned the importance of a compass. We sailed about 350 miles, and for part of that we were far enough out in the ocean that we couldn't see any land. When you can't see land it's a bit strange and scary. As you look around in all directions, all you see is water. It all looks the same. You can't tell by looking about you, which way to go to get anywhere. That's when you'd better have a compass. With a compass and a map you can go anywhere. On the trip we'd use the map to figure out the desired compass bearing. The person steering the boat would watch the compass and steer to hold the boat on that bearing. With just a compass bearing, you can reach a given destination and return.

The other thing that took on a new importance for me while cruising the Keys was all those buoys you find in offshore waters. Of course, many of the buoys near shore mark channels into harbors or mark shallow spots, but a lot of buoys are way out in the water, far from anything. Why are they there? To help boats navigate. They just help you figure out where you are. Our long journey was actually broken up into a series of trips from one buoy, or "marker," to the next. We'd use the map to figure the bearing to the next marker. As we got close, we'd start looking for it. When we got close enough, we'd note the number on the buoy to ensure that it was the one we were looking for. We'd write down the time we passed it. Then we'd repeat the process for the next marker. The paths between markers were basically straight, but looking at the overall route, it was clear that we went a little out of our way to go by those markers. Sailors do that. It's worth a little extra distance to have those periodic verifications that you're on the right track.

We need to have some guiding principles to give our life direction. Some things that matter to us; big things that make it worth all the little hassles. Some things to look forward to and to take pride in.

A man was visiting a home out in the country. As he drove into the driveway, he passed the barn. On the side of the barn were about a dozen targets with alternating red and white rings. An arrow was sticking out from the bullseye of each target. When he got to the house and met the occupant, he commented on the targets. He said, "You or someone here must be a really good archer, considering all those bulleyes."

The man replied, "Oh, that's easy. I shot the arrows, then painted the targets around them."

Do we establish our targets after the fact?

In the congregation of the church I belonged to as a teenager was a pair of old maid sisters. They were twins, and it was hard to tell them apart. They lived together and did everything together. I mean they were inseparable. Whenever you saw one the other was right beside her. We kids got a kick out of them. We thought they were really old, as teenagers think about lots of folks. Well, one of the sisters finally died. Naturally, a lot of people wondered how the second sister would get along without her, since they were so close. Know what happened? Within six months the second sister died. She didn't have any major health problems, she just died. I think she died of a lack of purpose. With her sister gone, she just didn't have enough reason to live to keep her alive.

Some scholars and writers have examined the lives of the people who were able to survive the horrible concentration camps in past wars. Viktor Frankl has written about a World War II camp at Auschwitz, Poland. The studies have shown that, almost to a person, those who survived had something important (to them) yet to do in their lives. They had something important to look forward to and to live for, and that kept them alive. Their enemies could inflict pain on them and damage their bodies, but as long as that driving force remained in their minds, they lived. Purpose kept them alive.

Beyond direction, we need a purpose. I think our purpose relates to success and happiness.

Psychologists are always conducting surveys to find out about people. I read about a survey they conducted to find out what makes people successful. They selected a large number of people who were considered "successful" in some endeavor, not necessarily employment. They covered as wide a range of endeavors as possible, then interviewed these people, trying to find any common threads that might indicate why they were successful. The people varied so much. The only common item they came up with was that these people were constantly taking on new challenges, learning and trying new things.

I read about another survey, conducted by a different group of psychologists. This one was aimed at finding out why people are happy. They selected a large group of people who had one thing in common: they appeared to others as being "happy." Beyond that trait, these people varied widely in every respect. The psychologists interviewed them, had them complete questionnaires, etc., to see if they could find any similarities. It was hard to identify trends. The only significant result was that these people were constantly taking on new challenges, learning and trying new things.

That's the same result as in the survey on "success." This means that the "approach to life" that leads to success is the same one that leads to happiness. Maybe it's not a coincidence. These two elements of our purpose in life—success and happiness—are evidently closely related.

Success is difficult to define, as I tried to explain earlier in this book. It doesn't relate to wealth or fame. It relates to one's contribution to the world, and that's something I've touched on in a number of chapters. It's spread throughout the book because one can be successful in so many different areas of life. We can be successful in our work, our family life, our community involvement, our relationships with other people, and other areas.

Here are a few more views on success:

"Self-trust is the first secret of success."—Emerson
(Back to the importance of self-esteem, right?)

"Success is focusing the full power of all you are on what you have a burning desire to achieve."—Wilferd A. Peterson

(Doesn't a "burning desire" sound like a purpose?)

To do for the world more than the world does for you— that is success."—Henry Ford

Happiness is also difficult to define. A problem here is that people tend to confuse happiness with fun. I discussed fun earlier and said that I think people need to have more fun. Fun is a day at the beach, the lake, or the amusement park. It's a party, a date, a ball game, or a movie. It's important, and it's particularly important that families have fun together. Lots of it.

Happiness is different than fun, but it's important, too. Happiness comes from things like achievement in work, a harmonious marriage, raising children, community involvement, commitment, and self-improvement. It comes from endeavors we tend to refer to as "rewarding." Happiness is a longer-term emotion than fun. It goes deeper.

Fun can be obtained relatively easily. You just do it. Happiness is much harder to achieve. It takes time, effort, and commitment. You can have fun while doing things that lead to happiness. But, ironically, the endeavors that lead to happiness usually involve some activities that most people would not consider fun. If we put the emphasis on carefree fun, happiness can elude us.

I've mentioned the Masons earlier. One offshoot of Masons is the Shrine organization. You've seen Shriners wearing their characteristic hats, probably in parades or at circuses. The Shrine is an interesting organization. It was originally formed from Masonry as a fun organization. The idea was to have lots of great parties and dances to be enjoyed by the members and their wives or guests. That's how it started out. But the Shriners soon found that all that fun was somehow hollow. They wanted to add some purpose to their organization, so they got into funding children's hospitals and other specialized hospitals, such as those for burn victims. Their system of great hospitals is now very widespread, and they're helping countless people every day. The Shrine circuses raise money for the hospitals. The Shriners still have a lot of fun, but they also know about happiness.

Here are a couple of other views:

"Not in doing what you like, but in liking what you do is the secret of happiness."—James M. Barrie

"To be without some of the things you want is an indispensable part of happiness."—Bertrand Russell

I remember that when I was a kid there was a time when I became concerned about dying. I guess I'd figured out that someday that would happen. I'd dream about it, then wake up crying, "I don't want to die." I got over it. Now I think if I have any concern about dying it's about what I should accomplish before my time comes. That's *purpose.*

I bet that when you were in high school you, like me, read Robert Frost's poem "Stopping by Woods on a Snowy Evening." It ends with the lines:

"But I have promises to keep
And miles to go before I sleep."

In high school I just thought he was a busy guy thinking about his "To Do" list and how tired he'd be before bedtime. But now I think he had something more general in mind. Do we ever think about what we really need to do or accomplish, and how far we really have to go in that respect, before our time is up? Maybe my high school English teacher would be proud of me, I'm not sure.

The key principles I've gleaned from my first half-century on this earth are, in a nutshell:

1. How we view ourselves and others, and hence how we treat others, determines what goes on with us and them.

2. We all have far more impact on others than we may realize, and we must be very aware and careful. Our impact is particularly great on young people, and greatest of all on any children we may be blessed to raise. We can easily increase our impact on others.

3. We are in complete control of our lives. That is a fact. The matter left to us is what we do with that control. We can relinquish it to others, or use it to accomplish what we wish.

4. Our happiness and success depend on applying ourselves to key principles in which we believe.

5. We're the product of all that we've done and seen. We never stop learning, and one of the most important ways we learn is by interacting with others.

6. The world is full of wonderful people.

I want to close by relating an incident that has had a profound impact on me:

I went to undergraduate school at the University of Cincinnati. In my field they had a co-op program in which, during the middle years of the curriculum, periods of school alternated with periods of work. The work provided good practical experience, helped us learn what engineering was all about, and helped us pay for college. My co-op job was with National Lead Company of Ohio. It was located about twenty five miles away from Cincinnati, so most of the employees who lived in Cincinnati carpooled to work. As soon as I started to work there, at the end of my freshman year, when I was eighteen, I got into a carpool. The carpool consisted of myself, another co-op student, and three men in their thirties and forties.

One day, during the first summer I worked there, the other co-op student was driving the carpool. On the way home from work we stopped at a produce stand beside the road because some of the men wanted to buy some corn. The next thing I remember from that trip home was when I was lying on the ground on my back. There was a blanket over me, and one place on my arm felt like it was cut. There were people standing around looking down at me, and when I tried to sit up they wouldn't let me. They said I should lie still.

Then I remember being loaded into an ambulance on a stretcher. I was put into the top on one side, like on the top of a bunk bed. Looking down on the other side, I saw on a stretcher one of the other men in the carpool. He had some blood on him. I heard some moaning from someone. Then I was in a hospital being examined. My mother appeared there to take me home.

Later I learned more about that fateful afternoon. The reason I had remembered so little was that I had *shock amnesia*, a common occurrence for accident victims. I guess the body tries to forget. Here's the rest of the story I was told:

The car was traveling along at highway speed when the driver evidently went to sleep or passed out. The car went off the side of the road and began to tip sideways as it got into the ditch beyond the shoulder. As it tilted close to ninety degrees, the top of the car hit a tree, which cut off the top of the car. Three of us were in the back seat; I was sitting behind the driver. This was in the days before cars had seat belts, and the three of us in the back seat were all thrown out of the car. I wasn't thrown too far. The other two men in the back seat were thrown much farther. One of them landed in a tree. They were both killed. The rest of us had only minor injuries. I had the cut on my arm (I can still find the scar as a reminder) and a couple of cracked ribs. Some time later I discovered a crack in one of my front teeth and a chip off another tooth, which I think were also results of the accident. One of the first things my mother said to me at the hospital was, "You were very lucky."

Among all my "scrapbook stuff," I have a yellowed copy of the article from the newspaper. It was on the front page. I also have a piece of red glass from a taillight of the car.

The death of those two men was very tragic. They each had four children, so eight children lost their fathers in that accident. We don't understand why such things happen. It's obviously very difficult for loved ones to come to terms with.

One thing I've thought about is how different things would be if I had died at that time, at the age of eighteen. My wife would have had to marry someone else. My three sons would not exist. My wife may have married someone else and had some other children, but not those three. They're unique individuals who got half their genes from each of us. Of course, I would have missed out on a lot over all these years.

Another thing I've thought about is, "Why didn't I die then?" I was sitting right next to the two men who did die. I think that incident gave me one of the most important principles affecting my life. You see, I think I was spared because God had some things in mind for me to do before calling me home. Maybe it was to give something to a wonderful woman, or to three young men, or to some other people I've passed by or traveled with for a spell along this journey. I don't know.

I think God puts us all here on Earth to accomplish some things. Some of these things may come naturally to us during the course of our lives. Other things we need to seek out and do. How can we find out what tasks we're supposed to accomplish? Maybe by experimenting; by watching for opportunities; by trying a lot of things that we think might be part of the plan, and seeing what seems to "click."

What kind of plans do you think God has made for you?

Best wishes in fulfilling those plans! When tough things come your way and you find yourself asking, "Why me?" remember that maybe it's because God needed someone with special talents for a difficult task. Maybe He's counting on you.

I don't know what I'll be doing after I leave this Earth, but until that time comes I know what I'll keep striving to do. I'll work hard, play hard, enjoy my family, help others, enjoy the world, keep fit, give thanks, and have fun. I'll strive to focus on others and treat them with respect. Through that, I'll strive to fulfill my divine purpose here, my own unique form of success and happiness. I hope you will too. God bless you.

Author's Note

At one of these places where they show old-time crafts, a man was carving on a very ornate wooden door. A woman watching thought the door looked finished and that what the man was doing was at a very fine detail level. So she asked him, "How do you know when the door is finished?"

He replied, "It's never finished. After a while they just come and take it away."

The only negative aspect of publishing this book is that I have to stop working on it. I've been writing it for over ten years, off and on. Writing it has been enjoyable. And, of course, I've been "collecting" material for it all my life, most of the time not even knowing I was doing so. I want to thank the innumerable people who have in one way or another given me something that I've been able to pass on to you in this book. I couldn't possibly identify even a significant fraction of them.

I certainly hope that this book has been helpful and entertaining to you. I hope it truly makes a difference for you, because it deals with what I think is the most profound aspect of living, that is, how we impact others. This book is one way I'm striving to make a difference, and I know you, too, will find ways to make a difference with others.

REFERENCES

1. Carnegie, Dale, *How to Win Friends and Influence People*, Pocket Books, 98th printing, 1973.

2. Helmstetter, Shad, *What to Say When You Talk to Yourself*, Thorsons, p. 41, 1991.

3. Carnegie, Dale, *How to Win Friends and Influence People*, Pocket Books, 98th printing, p. 102, 1973.

4. Covey, Steven., *The Seven Habits of Highly Effective People*, Simon & Schuster, p. 30, 1994.

5. Carnegie, Dale, *How to Win Friends and Influence People*, Pocket Books, 98th printing, p. 21, 1973.

6. ibid, p. 28.

7. ibid, p. 36.

8. Oursler, Fulton., There is Magic in a Word of Praise, *Reader's Digest*, August 1952.

9. Carnegie, Dale, *How to Win Friends and Influence People*, Pocket Books, p. 62, 98th printing, 1973.

10. Chase, Stuart, *The Power of Words*, Harcourt Brace and Co. Also Are You Listening in *Getting the Most Out of Life*, The Reader's Digest Association, p. 237, 1955.

11. Fear, Richard A., *The Evaluation Interview*, McGraw-Hill Book Co., 3rd edition, 1984.

Keys to Effective Interpersonal Relationships

1. Focus on others

2. Recognize the extreme importance of self-esteem (the other person's!)

3. The way people act depends on how we expect them to act

4. Instead of criticizing others' behavior, try to understand why they behave as they do

5. The only kind of motivation that really works and lasts is self-motivation

6. Keep a positive and enthusiastic attitude, and pass it on to everyone you can

7. Seek opportunities to praise, show appreciation, and encourage others

8. Be actively considerate of others

9. Be sure you really know the human resources you deal with, and make the most of them

10. Seize opportunities to help others by coaching and mentoring

11. Create the kind of communication atmosphere that's most effective for accomplishing your objectives, and that's usually an open, honest one

12. Be the kind of pleasant, positive, smiling, courteous person others enjoy being around

Keys to Effective Communications

1. Choose carefully the communication mode you use: face-to-face, by telephone, by e-mail, or in writing

2. Listen carefully to others, and let them know you're listening

3. Be sure the questions you ask serve your real objective, which includes building rapport

4. Be sure the non-verbal messages you send fit your purpose

5. Make the meetings you arrange effective, and be an effective participant in every meeting you attend

6. Whether you're speaking or writing, think about what your audience wants

7. Practice a talk more than you think is necessary, and get the timing right

8. Make your writing as clear and concise as possible

About the Author

Doug Hissong grew up in Ohio, and obtained his undergraduate and graduate education in engineering at the University of Cincinnati and Ohio State University, respectively. He has worked in research and engineering companies in Ohio, New Jersey, Louisiana, and Texas.

He now lives in Houston. He is married and has three sons (of whom he is very proud). His leisure interests include water skiing and snow skiing.

Cedar Fort, Incorporated
Order Form

Name:_____

Address: _____

City: _____ State: _____ Zip: _____

Phone: (   ) _____ Daytime phone: (   ) _____

Positive Impacts

Quantity: _____ @ $14.95 each: _____

plus $3.49 shipping & handling for the first book: _____

(add 99¢ shipping for each additional book)

Utah residents add 6.25% for state sales tax: _____

                                        TOTAL: _____

Mail this form and payment to:

Cedar Fort, Inc.

925 North Main St.

Springville, UT 84663

You can also order on our website **www.cedarfort.com**

or e-mail us at sales@cedarfort.com or call 1-800-SKYBOOK

9 26575 75821 7